CHANGING THE GUARD

Other books by Dan Hardy

**THE COMPLETE POOL MANUAL FOR HOMEOWNERS
AND PROFESSIONALS**
A Step-by-Step Maintenance Guide
"Winner of 4 Awards"

THE COMPLETE SPA MANUAL FOR HOMEOWNERS
A Step-by-Step Maintenance and Therapy Guide

RUNNING FROM MY SHADOW
My Own Worst Enemy

CHANGING THE GUARD

Taking Back America

By Dan Hardy

iUniverse, Inc.
New York   Bloomington

Changing the Guard
Taking Back America

Copyright © 2010 by Dan Hardy

This is a work of fiction. All of the characters, names, incidents, organizations, and dialogue in this novel are either the products of the author's imagination or are used fictitiously.

iUniverse books may be ordered through booksellers or by contacting:

iUniverse
1663 Liberty Drive
Bloomington, IN 47403
www.iuniverse.com
1-800-Authors (1-800-288-4677)

ISBN:
ISBN:

Printed in the United States of America

iUniverse rev. date: 12/15/2009

This book is dedicated to all of the concerned citizens of the United States of America that has inspired this book to come from a simple idea to an actual creation. We all long for the day when our government returns to the job and represents the citizens where we will once again be represented by the officials that have been elected and demand that we are not ignored and called names.

CONTENTS

▼

Introduction

United States of America was in turmoil. The new administration was geared for personal gain and not a thought was given to the every day Americans that work, pay taxes, and support our economy. The beneficiaries of the financial plan from the White House were geared for organizations that simply would provide the politicians with their vote. We had turned into a Socialist state.

Special interest groups, large lobbying firms, and just about anyone important that wanted to own a politician could do so with a simple contribution. The current Democratic administration had made sure that the Justice Department was not going to prosecute any politician for taking money from some individual or organization.

Fear was setting in that the President was trying to cut more of the military so additional money would be in circulation for his own private policies. Terrorist all over the world were just waiting for the big military cut so they could join forces and take over the United States. Our allies were scared and even rumors had surfaced that Israel might assassinate our president to get new leadership.

It came time that Americans would use the Constitution the way it was intended to take control of the country and regain a democratic society and stop the socialism that was being forced on everyone. We had to take control before the Constitution was amended so bad that it would not be feasible to challenge the current government. It was time to *Change the Guard*. And to do it was so simple because our military was not in the United States in great force but overseas. The current Executive and Legislative Branches were so involved with their own greed, they overlooked the warning signs. That in itself was not unusual because the lawmakers had ignored their duties for years and had gotten us into a mess with our economy and our value of the dollar was worthless.

Changing of the Guard is not only an interesting story but possibly could be in the planning stages in reality. Could it actually happen in America? If something doesn't change we may see the new Presidential Seal say The United Socialist States of America.

This is a fictional based story and is not intended to be a plan to over take our government. It is solely for entertainment purposes and not to be taken seriously. The author and publisher believe the way to actually **Change the Guard** is in the voting booth.

CHAPTER 1

▼

OUR DAMAGED COUNTRY

This story did not come to light by me thinking about a good story. In reality it came from the public. Occasionally we all have listened to some hotshot that will make a comment like having a revolution, but not often. But as the problems increase here in the United States I start hearing it more and more from the average American. So I decided to play a small game. I will pose as an author in the attempt to get information about a new book. I am an author but really I did not have plans to write a book about this subject.

This idea came to me because my wife wanted to spend some time in St. Augustine, Florida. It is a beautiful city with a multitude of history. But, I see something once and it is not very exciting the second time. I thought while she is looking through all the little shops in the historic part of the city, I will mingle and try to get people to express their opinion about our failing government. Tourists from all over the United States go to St. Augustine, and I think that I can get a good sense of how the country sees our current situation. I am not prepared for what I hear.

Our present Presidential administration started out very popular and we all wished them the best. But it did not take long before the public was getting discouraged and angry over policies, and the failure to use the Legislative Branch of our government to introduce laws. Instead a very ingenious way of bypassing them came about. Using executive orders and appointing Czars, that do not require Congressional approval, is the name of the game. Many can see changing our present way of government to Socialism, or even a Dictatorship is what concerns most of the people I talk to. The promise to not raise taxes has definitely become a joke, and many people are afraid that the government is going to open up shop as the nations bankers, stockbrokers, car manufacturers, insurance agents, and health care providers. This scares many people. Citizens that understand government and how their involvement affects things do not like the idea of officials taking control of these industries and many more.

What the country does understand, is the damage that bribery disguised as legitimate money from lobbyist and special interests groups, has literally changed most of our politicians. There was a time when a politician had money and he or she had come to office with that money. Politics are not profitable. Now people cannot wait to get elected to become rich. It is not uncommon for a politician to become a millionaire in the first term of office from the funds they receive from lobbyists that represent different organizations. These organizations have one thing in mind and that is to own a politician. Owning a politician lets them get the needed bill passed.

This book has two purposes. The first purpose, you will not hear from most authors, but I am not the typical establishment author. It is simply to sell a good book that most will enjoy by spending their down time utilizing their mind and being entertained. The belief that because one publishes a book they are automatically rich is far from the truth. But in order to make some money and not waste my time, I need to produce a product that is entertaining, possibly educational, and for this book, I want people to become more aware of their surroundings especially on the political side. Lord knows that the school systems of America are not doing a very good job at educating our younger people to facts, and not a predetermined political agenda. Our colleges are not teaching the subjects, but let teachers and professors preach their political beliefs, and many times they intimidate the students to believe the way they do, or fail the class. The second purpose of this book is to let the public and our leaders know that the public is tired of the way things are going and the last thing that many want is to become a state where they are told what to do and when to do it.

I chose this subject because there are a lot of people talking about revolution, and sometimes more dangerous thinking is going on. Again if it is a subject many have on their minds, then they are potential customers that may purchase this book, but also it really is a subject that is on the minds of many Americans. Change originally sounds good to some. But the type of change is what concerns many. As Americans we hear of a change of something and we get excited about it because the policies that are currently implemented are not exactly what the public wants. But in all of this excitement we forget to ask the important question; how is the government going to change this? So we vote for the change and then it hits us hard that the change we voted for, is not what we had in mind. This happens every election so it is not a new subject. Many times, we as voters, are lied to just to vote for the individual that promises these changes. And this too happens every election. If one thing is for sure voters cannot believe what they are promised, but yet we are too busy to take time and research an individual or agency. We just fall into that same old procedure to trust. So for those people who feel that they voted for the wrong crooks, I mean politicians, you have gotten what you deserve. There is no place in the voting booth for ignorance. If you decide to listen to the news agencies instead of your own research, then that makes you worse than ignorant.

Changing The Guard is a book of imagination that has stemmed from conversations with many people. Some of those conversations have resulted in words that I can never print. If I do I will have black SUV's park outside of my house with little men with dark glasses on at night and telephone cords sticking out of their ears.

The thought of a revolution or coup is not new to America. But very few Americans know of the biggest peacetime threat to American democracy. The entire episode was dismissed so that the idea would just disappear and not be talked about. Ultimately it was more involved than what the government wanted the average American to know, and this deeply scared many politicians. During the depression half-a-million war veterans were to assist in a plot to topple President Franklin D. Roosevelt. Some say many of the most powerful business people and families were behind this coup.

Business Plot (also the **Plot Against FDR** and the **White House Putsch**) was an alleged political conspiracy in 1933 which involved wealthy businessmen plotting a coup d'état to overthrow United States President Franklin D. Roosevelt. In 1934 retired Marine Corps Major General Smedley Butler testified to the McCormack-Dickstein Congressional Committee that a group of men had approached him as part of a plot to overthrow Roosevelt in a coup. One of the purported plotters, Gerald MacGuire, vehemently denied any such plot. In their report, the Congressional committee stated that it was able to confirm Butler's statements other than the proposal from MacGuire. However, no prosecutions or further investigations followed. Some historians have questioned whether or not a plot was actually close to execution. Contemporary media dismissed the plot with *The New York Times* characterizing it as a *gigantic hoax.*

Roosevelt was trying to get the New Deal passed. To get this bill passed Roosevelt agreed that the plotters would walk free if Wall Street would back off of the opposition to the New Deal and let FDR do what he wanted. The investigations into the coup disappeared when it was time for everyone to testify against each other. It was covered up.

Our Constitution is being played with right now. It is being bent, folded, tested, and abused by many of our elected officials. Many ignore the laws and proceed with their own ideas making things up as they go. Many feel that they are above the law, and they should because there are very few people and agencies, that are going to enforce these broken laws and policies. We have seen this before but in our troubled time now, it is as if our politicians are rubbing our noses in it, and they are flaunting the corrupt policies in our faces.

I hope you enjoy this book and the next time we are getting close to an election, do some research, and do not follow the crowd because it seems popular. Again I want to make it clear that even with all the people I have listened to, I still believe that the right way to **Change The Guard** is in the voting booth. But many have limited patience.

Chapter 2

▼

The Beginning of Dangerous Thinking

My name is Steve Taylor. I am just an average Middle American worker trying to provide for my family. I primarily worked construction for most of my life. Jobs come and go and steady employment is getting harder to get. It is the beginning of 2011 and we are fixing to have another crooked election. The same old lies are being promised. We have learned from our last election that promises are cheap and greed rules.

I opened my own business several years ago and do residential handiwork. I do miscellaneous repairs on homes mainly for the retired. I have a good reputation and am known as a man of many trades but a master of none. That means that I do a lot of different things but I am not real talented as most professionals. My work is good but there is plenty of competition. I am honest and I give my customers what they want, with very few complaints, or at least none that I cannot fix.

What is said about me is that I am dependable, sober, and show up when I tell them I will. If I ever get delayed, the customer will always get a call letting them know. I am known to not charge anyone for things that were not done and never charge anyone for something that did not come out right, making sure before I leave I have a satisfied customer.

I do many things such as fence repair, sheetrock repair and painting, and residential plumbing and occasionally some electrical repairs. Most of the jobs I do are out of my occupational license scope, but people are glad that they do not have to call several different people. Especially when it is almost impossible for them to get people to show up for the scheduled appointment.

Until I moved to Florida I had never seen such terrible business practices as I've seen here. It is like every service related person has more money than they need and just keeps appointments if they are close to the local bar or VFW that is in that particular area. All I have to do is just show up for the appointment and usually get the job if I feel I can do it properly.

Before I started this business I was a realtor for a few years. When the housing boom came my wife and I cleaned up. When it crashed, so did we, and we have to be very creative to keep our family above water and keep the bills paid and our stomachs full. Sometimes it has become pretty hard and we live from paycheck to paycheck. We have no health insurance and we are barely able to keep up our automotive insurance so that we will be able to drive. It never fails that when we start to get ahead and save some money something will happen and it cost us all that we have in reserve and then some. All the promises that we were told with the previous election were naturally all lies. Same lies but we keep our hopes up that this time it will be different.

I started becoming very frustrated and really needed to talk about my feelings with other people but that went against my policy. I have a policy that as a businessman I do not discuss politics, religion or abortion. These are the subjects that deal with personal feelings and you normally cannot change a persons' mind or view, and usually it upsets them. I have lost a few jobs by my discussions so I feel it is better to not talk about these subjects with my customers.

I really became upset when I tried to trade in my truck for a newer one. I learned that because the government has forced the vehicle manufacturer to close dealerships and turn more control over to the unions, my vehicle has dropped in value rapidly. From having good equity in the truck I am now upside down. Everything that I use has tax increases and the products have risen in price substantially. With the economy the way it is, it is hard to pass on these increases to my clients.

One day a new client still has a sign from the previous election with the names of the losing presidential candidates, that I voted for in his garage. Frustrated I just opened my mouth and asked him, "What do you think we would be going through if they had gotten elected?" I should have honored my own policy because this man started expressing his opinion and it was not a quick conversation.

He is a fairly wealthy man and I am really amazed that with our economy in the sewer that he is having difficulties. He has lost a great deal of money since the stock market went to crap in 2008. Then the new lawmakers raised taxes, deleted many deductions that the average businessman incurred running a business, and made working for one self very difficult, if you do it by the law and are honest in your tax preparation. It seems more and more every day that our government is penalizing more small businesses. They have raised the capitol gains taxes so much that it is hard to make a profit. It appears that no member of our government has actually paid taxes and has gotten away with things that the average individual cannot do.

It has become so bad, because the federal government has used most of the revenues for the personal gain of the elected officials and their little pork-spending request, that money to the states has been cut short. When the states have no money, they give less to the counties, and then the cities are left short. Some are in serious financial problems. The local governments cut teachers, law enforcement, and fire fighters. Our most needed people are put out of work and are partly the reason why our unemployment rate is so high. Crime is increasing daily so some people can acquire money to feed their family.

To counter the problem, property taxes have gone totally out of sight. Gas prices rose because the states, as well as the federal government, have imposed additional taxes to try and increase revenue to fund these many different agendas. Public utilities cost have increased so much that we use our hurricane lamps at night a lot to save on electricity expense. I am even worried about flushing the toilet because the price of water has increased so much. For those that cannot quit smoking, the price of cigarettes is so high that it causes problems with daily survival. Many people have bought bare land and placed a recreational vehicle on the property to live in so they will not have enormous taxes.

The unions have turned back into the same organizations that they were when Al Capone was in charge of things in Chicago. All the pension funds have disappeared. The dues that are mandatory have increased to about twenty percent of a member's paycheck going back to the union. The secret vote within the union has been abolished. This allows the union officials to terrorize the members of their union if they lean toward voting for a plan that is not favorable for the high- ranking members of the union. The politicians put up with the unions because they can guarantee a large amount of people to vote for the Democratic Party. People still vote that way even though no one will help them or rescue them from the extortion that the unions demand. The leaders use some Union people to intimidate people at town hall meetings and in some cases assault some of them. The political process has turned into a gang style activity. Even though "freedom of speech" is our right, some pay dearly for voicing their opinion. Fear tactics for politicians are being used more and more and those who stand up for their rights are often punished.

Wal-Mart stores started closing their doors because Congress made Wal-Mart accept the union in. To cover the expenses of the union wages, prices of items are no longer a bargain and so many employees have lost their jobs and benefits. Rumors are that Wal-Mart is going to sell their stores to a non-union retailer. That is causing people to protest and boycott Wal-Mart.

What people have not considered is when Wal-Mart started opening stores all over the country they ran the Mom and Pop stores out of business. Now when a Wal-Mart store in a particular town shut its' doors, then most towns have limited places to shop, and it has become hard to find many items. Internet shopping is on the rise but the government started putting a tax on these purchases as well as a tax for an individual to use the Internet. Uncle Sam has become a watchdog against the people instead of a source of security.

To make matters worse there is a business operational tax that raises with the increase sales a store makes. It is usually easier on the storeowners and sometimes more profitable to stay small and keep limited inventory. With an additional increase in the inventory tax, most shop owners do not want any inventory when tax time comes around. Overall it is getting real bad. In addition many companies have chosen not to expand and so new jobs are not being established. Kids getting out of high school and even college cannot find a job because there are none.

Taxes have risen so high on firearms and the government has put so many restrictions on gun owners that many people are buying guns on the black market. There finally are more guns smuggled into the country than drugs. Ammunition is getting harder to buy and when you do purchase ammunition you had to state the reason for the purchase and present your drivers license. This is recorded and reported to the Federal Government. If you buy enough ammunition that someone can consider it excessive, you might get a visit from some ATF agent. Under the new laws a federal officer can come to your house at any time to inspect weapons that you have bought legally and look for illegal weapons.

The borders that surrounded the United States are a joke. With the cuts that Congress has enacted most of the Border Patrol agents have been laid off. We have people coming from all over the world walking right up the freeway in California and Texas. Many people come from Canada. This is great for the gun smugglers. Many gun manufacturers opened factories in other countries. They supply guns to be brought over the border. The Mexican government does not care because it is good revenue for them.

We have people killing each other all of the time. Muslims killing Jews. Jews killing Muslims. Catholics are attacked and churches are being burnt down. The Baptist Churches finance militias to protect their members. Skinheads are everywhere. Crossbows started appearing in many murders because of the lack of noise and lack of government restrictions. Pipe bombs are used more and more for gang assassinations. It has turned into one big free-for-all for violence.

Pro-active policing is almost gone by local law enforcement agencies. They are loosing too many officers and the police departments have backed off of fighting crime just to stay alive. The courts can get bought off so easy that many arrested individuals simply pay the courts like bail money to have their cases dropped. Anyone with a little money can own a state attorney or a judge. It is pretty much like it was in the early 2000's with the exception that it takes less money to buy your freedom.

Cubans can actually take a cruise ship to Mexico and buses take them across the border into California. Once they arrive into the United States they are automatically Democratic voters and are protected. In Miami it is almost impossible to find an English speaking person. We have hoped that many of the Cuban refugees would go back to Cuba once the restrictions were lifted, but they chose just to go visit relatives and return.

The big promise that we all hear from the politicians is healthcare. This has been used as a political campaign lie for 30 years and less people have healthcare at this time then ever recorded. Doctors are becoming scarce. Socialized medicine has all but killed the medical profession. The ones that stay in it are poorly paid and poorly trained. You will be better off finding a good Veterinarian if you want quality medical treatment. American healthcare has been destroyed and no one knows how to fix it. The politicians just point their fingers at the other side and the voters. They blame the failure of a healthcare plan on the voters.

The pharmaceutical manufacturers have taken control of the entire over the counter medications and it takes a prescription to get an Advil or Vitamins. People have turned to growing their own herbs for medicinal purposes. The smuggling of medications is almost as lucrative as firearms smuggling. Many herbal treatment centers have opened up to help treat people of illnesses and injuries. These of course are run underground just like a Speak Easy was run during prohibition.

Americans that do have money eventually got tired of the taxes on their money and have left the country. Naturally there are heavy taxes for removing your money from American banks but it is less expensive than staying in America and paying the outrageous taxes and levies. It is funny but many people bought land in Mexico and moved down there. Many moved to Canada.

The news agencies are mainly government propaganda like a communist country. The Fairness Doctrine was re-enacted and talk shows are almost all gone because people do not want to listen to liberal shows and their views so the radio and television stations can not afford to host both. If you want to hear conservative talk shows then you have to have a satellite radio. The entertainment industry has turned political and every entertainer has a mission and an opinion. Newspapers have all but disappeared so news is heard on the national propaganda stations.

Community holiday decorations are gone because it offends too many foreigners, which are Democratic voters. Some cities made it illegal to have Christmas decorations that can be seen from the outside of your home. It is illegal to smoke in your house in some cities. Employers have to provide special prayer places and honor certain time for religious nuts from other places. It is against the law to talk in a manner that is not political correct. Churches are used often to pass on political agendas and information. Only as long as it is within a specific political party line.

The best business to be in is a small one-man business where you can hide money that you earned to avoid the high taxes. I do a lot of services for barter. It is like the old days. I did work for a pig that the customer butchered for me. We worked for half a steer and trade services for many chickens. People are always coming up with more ideas to hide income to avoid the high taxes.

Politics is so criminal that it is often funny. Congress has enacted a law that made them exempt from federal taxes. They claim that it is a conflict of interest to vote on issues concerning taxes. So to eliminate the conflict, they just eliminated taxes imposed on each other. The citizens complain but the politicians do not care about our thoughts. It has turned into socialism on a grand scale. Votes are bought in advance so that if one has an issue with one of their representatives, complaining to them does not matter. It is a situation where an elected official no longer listens to the people who voted for them. Rumor is that the elections are all fixed anyway so it does not matter if you vote for them or not.

I am able to continue and work but have changed my routines quite a bit because fuel prices have risen to over five dollars a gallon for gasoline. I have a large garden where I raise most of my vegetables. Due to my high cholesterol vegetables are good for me and we eat well and trade vegetables with our neighbors. What meat we do not barter for we can buy from independent butcher shops. From the work I do for one of my customers, I always have a few chickens in the freezer.

Even though we have what we need, it still is the idea that our government is failing the people and our foreign policy is an absolute train wreck. When I do turn on the news it is the same thing. One-sided propaganda on how great America is and how powerful a nation we are. In reality we are not that powerful anymore and every time someone decides we need to cut some expense it comes out of our military and homeland security.

In all fairness we are becoming a joke to the other nations of the world and everyone knows that it is only a matter of time before some nation attacks us again. We are in three wars at this time. Iraq is still going on but is more like a mopping up police action. Afghanistan is a hot bed for terrorism but somehow one of our big bombers made a terrible mistake and took out most of the terrorists that were located on the Afghanistan and Pakistan border. The plane was loaded with some new type of bomb and killed thousands of militants. Our government apologized and then everyone celebrated because it surely was a great thing to eliminate so many high level terrorists.

The war we started with Iran is not a big issue since we do not have troops on the ground. We will lob a few rockets at them on occasions, and they are in a real mess. The infrastructure is gone and the citizens have no running water or electricity. The world leaders think that we are abusive for attacking and almost destroying a country for attacking one of our planes. They damned us to the media and then come over here for discussions and enjoy what we have to offer. Our government will bomb the leaders of Iran one day and then celebrate with them on the next day. New York city has become a place for all of the terrorist and bad people to come and spend their money. They are protected here as long as their money does not run out.

Our politicians have become host for every country we hate and are a threat to our great nation. No country takes us seriously anymore because they know they too can own an American politician with a few bucks. Buying American lawmakers has become more profitable than a whorehouse in Las Vegas. Greed has taken over instead of loyalty and duty. The values of our leaders have faded away and it can be compared to an auction. The highest bidder wins no matter what the effect of their actions does to the people of this country.

We are loosing some of our best military leaders. They cannot stand to see what is going on with our country. The limitations that are put on them make their job almost impossible. They choose to retire instead of sending our soldiers into situations where they can no longer fight without first going over a checklist provided by the civilian authorities of our country. Congress and other leaders cannot let the military do something that might affect the upcoming election by making someone other than a natural born American angry. It is not uncommon for our military personnel to leave our country and work for another that pays them well and lets them do their job. Many times they are fighting against the United States. So our government set up death squads within the CIA to eliminate these people that change sides.

When I was out in the public arena I began to listen to people describe how disgusted they are with our situation. More than one time I have heard people express their idea that we should just march up to Washington D.C. and take over control. I hear this from not only the everyday person but also law enforcement, bankers, doctors, current and ex-military people. The opinions expressed on some of the talk shows that are left are the same. Editorials in the daily papers, that are still in existence, express the same ideas and our leaders do nothing. They are so involved with making money and new friends that they ignore the warning signs the people are expressing. It is the first time that people who have money are really disgusted with their situation and are offering a lot of money to help end this madness and socialistic ideas.

As time pass I can hear ideas on how to take back control of our country and get it out of the hands of the crooks that are in charge. I have become interested in these ideas that I am hearing and I am so surprised by them. If we go on a short trip on the weekend I will mingle where people gather and listen to their ideas and opinions. It is not uncommon to have someone of power involved in this conversation. I started making a list of people that I hear voicing their opinion that we need to do something. At this time I really do not know why, but I want to see how many people feel the same way that I do. As time passes I have a list of people that can exceed the current voting registration.

As I compile my list I notice that the government people and the union people are the only ones that are halfway satisfied. Middle America has been lied to and they are worse off than they have been in many years. Even the rich are having difficulties, if they are not involved in the spreading of their wealth to our leaders. The illegal immigrants are allowed to run around the country. There are limited programs to help them but many return to their native country. Many of them set up illegal enterprises and are able to exploit the honest Americans. Help from law enforcement is very limited.

We started seeing frustration being taken out on government buildings, vehicles, and the infrastructure. We have bombings of buildings, mostly on a small scale and no big bombs. Bank robberies are a daily occurrence and some are robbed almost daily. Molotov cocktails are being thrown at government vehicles whether they are federal, state, or municipality owned. All kinds of things are being sent through the mail to our leaders from powdery substances to body parts of animals and some human parts. Kidnappings from foreigners are on the rise and really no one is safe.

This intense frustration caused the KKK and the Arian Nation to expand in membership and they have become active again. But this time it is not geared so much at the minorities but at the government. Militants from all races are becoming more active. One night on the evening news they had a video of a known KKK leader and the leader of a black militant group talking on the street in Chicago. The news report stated that this is people from all different ways of life getting along and how great America has become. In many ways this is correct but not for the reason the media tries to convey to the public. They are combining their forces to be strong whenever they are needed to combat something that upsets them.

The crime rate has risen so high and there are so many home invasions and burglaries that local law enforcement is unable to keep up. This is happening all over the country but in greater numbers in the big cities. The criminal elements have learned that it is better to stay in larger cities then to come out to rural America. The stupid ones will wander to small towns and communities and it is not uncommon to find them shot or even hung by the neck for stealing. Smaller communities stick together like a family and each resident watches out for strangers and unusual activities that are not normal in their area.

Because of some of the new laws that have been enacted citizens feared reporting crime to the police because they can confiscate weapons and other things upon their investigation of the reported crime. Some people loose more things from the police confiscation then what the burglar has taken. Because of this situation many crimes are not reported, and if a thief is caught, many times the community will deal with the criminal. Small kangaroo courts have become somewhat common in the rural areas. This is done mainly as entertainment because all thieves are killed. Some of the dead bodies of these criminals are actually delivered to their home as a reminder that crime does not pay in some areas.

It is not uncommon for the police to get reports of dead bodies laying by the roadside in their jurisdiction. If a thief is shot then instead of taking a chance of reporting the crime, the homeowner will just haul the body someplace and dump it. The authorities will just pick up the body like a dead animal and haul it away. Very little investigation is usually done when a criminal is found dead.

An activity that started in rural Vermont and northern New York State is that thieves will watch shoppers at grocery stores. When the items are loaded in the car the bad guys will simply follow the person home, which usually is a woman, and rob them as they get home. Once they are at your home they will take more, and rapes and murders have increased during this activity. As the news agencies report these crimes, this same scenario has spread across the country.

Some communities will travel in caravans to the stores for protection and always have armed men and women to accompany them. Many vigilante types will watch for cars following their residents and will take whatever action they want to when they determined that these individuals have plans of robbing, or just documenting information about a property that they went to. The thieves are sophisticated in that they may not rob a woman taking her groceries home at that time but will video tape the property to provide them with information so that they can return later to commit the crime. Groups of people are caught doing just this but they are selling the tapes to other criminals to provide them with a place to rob and details of the property. They too have been found executed.

Usually when an individual arrives home they will let any dogs out that they have. This is good information. A dog is dangerous plus noisy and can alert neighbors. Dogs being poisoned are not uncommon. Some of these information gatherers do such a good job of gathering information, they have the time the residents go to work and where they work. They will compile details of what people do as a routine. This information provides whoever is going to rob a residence with very valuable information for the thief that does not want to commit a cold call robbery.

Another common practice of thieves is they will look for homes that are for sale that have a virtual tour on the Internet. A good virtual tour can be enhanced and one can see what items are in their home and the basic layout. The video will provide information on security such as alarms or sliding glass doors that do not have good locking mechanisms. The other thing will be to make an appointment with the realtor and meet them at the home, and then rob the home and the agent. Many real estate agents are hurt, raped, or robbed. It has become such a common practice that some municipalities will have police escorts go along with a realtor to show a home.

A large theft ring will actually meet an agent to look at a home and when the thieves feel that the agent is comfortable with their intentions of wanting to purchase a home, then they will call someone and a truck will appear. While the agent is there, the neighbors think that everything is okay and pay little attention to what is going on. Usually the virtual tour will show the surrounding neighborhood and one can see if homes are close together or if it is a house that is hard to see due to trees or other obstructions. Some real estate agents are even caught selling the tour videos to thieves. It has become a very sophisticated business.

Not only has America become a dangerous place to live but also due to our legislative branch de-regulating many things, prices have risen to where a young couple can not support their family. Multiple families living under one roof is becoming more common. This creates a rise in domestic violence.

Children are being home schooled. Unfortunately many that do home school their kids are uneducated and what they are producing is an uneducated and ignorant individual. Watching these children upsets me because these are our future leaders and it has come to my attention that we as a country are going to be in a bad situation when they get older. The role model our kids are watching is very bad. Our own leaders and the media seemed to have an agenda to promote corruption. They are giving our children bad influence.

It is time that something is done about this situation. I know that we have to change the direction and leadership of our country but I do not know how to do it. I had no idea how to proceed until one day I watched an old news clip of a march on Washington D.C. called The Million Man March. I thought to myself how easy it would be to take over the government if these million people had been armed. From that thirty-second news clip came the idea that led to the upcoming situation.

At first I felt that it is an impossible situation but I am curious to see how many people will actually be committed to participating in a venture as dangerous as this. I am totally surprised by the enormous support people have to rid our government of these criminals.

One of the amazing facts that startled me is the amount of support that the government has from certain people. I cannot understand why they will support such criminal activity from our leaders. Are they getting a small portion of the pot by participating in the ideas of our leaders? Are they promised an exclusive piece of property that the government will steal from some poor average citizen? Or are they just stupid? It is a question that I cannot answer. It is a question that some of the participants cannot answer. Many feel that it is just the way it is suppose to be. This feeling changed when I listened to a commercial later that day. There is a meeting of poor people at one of our unused sports arenas. This lady is saying that she is there to get money from our president. She has no sense on where he is getting the money and thinks that there is a special fund for lazy, poor, and definitely stupid people. As I listen to her I realize that some people actually believe that a promise used in one of the campaigns is really going to happen and our new president will hand out money just because of their minority status. How disappointed she is that money handouts are not really happening that way.

At the end of the day it does not really matter. Unless something is going to be done to stop or change the way things are going our country is heading right toward the toilet. Many times it is a blessing to not watch or hear any news of the day. It only makes things worse. It has been along time since I have actually heard a good news report that has a happy ending. The mainstream media does not report on good events. It almost seems as if there is a race to see which organization can report the most tragic news that they can find. The weather report seems to be the most exciting news for me.

Even though the politicians seem to ignore the average American there has been an agency formed that monitors the social sites of the Internet. Rumor has it a list is being compiled against people that routinely make subversive comments. It reminds me of the time that J. Edgar Hoover used to keep files on the Beatles and other rock groups. Spying on the public must have been a form of entertainment for some. All-though I have never known someone that has gotten into trouble for their comments or thoughts. but one cannot take a chance. I do use the social sites a lot but I just keep my thoughts to myself and avoid answering questions concerning the government and their policies. It is hard sometimes to keep my thoughts to myself but I force myself. I also stay away from sites that may be controversial. I learned that if I want to research something that may have been seen as trouble, I go to the library and use their computers. But the last time I was at the library there was a man that just walked around the library especially where the computers are. He looked over to see the monitor as if he was spying on the users. I believe I am paranoid.

CHAPTER 3

▼

THE PLANNING STAGE

When I decided that we have to do something about our political situation, I also know that I have to be very careful and not advertise my idea. I have no idea that I will ever do anything, or get anything organized, but it seems to occupy my mind and that makes me less angry because I have a mission to concentrate on. If my idea of changing our leaders or even trying to organize a march intended to get the attention of our politicians became public, I may never be seen again.

My original idea is to organize a march on Washington and once there, bring up the idea that if our leaders do not do their job and stop all the personal gain programs they are involved with, they can easily be removed from office by force. For some reason many people that have the same idea as I do, are the exact ones that keep voting in these thieves and non-productive individuals to our leadership.

Our sitting President has not fulfilled his campaign promises and spends most of the time overseas making friends and giving away our country to foreign leaders, that are not our friends. But they are glad to accept our money and technology. It is worse than when the previous administrations were in the White House. All of this has to come to an end. Our own population needs reform and we need to create new jobs to get our economy back strong, instead of giving it away to foreign leaders.

Even planning a simple march like this can be seen as trying to overthrow the government, and the dangers of being locked up for the rest of my life is a possibility. So I have to do this in a way that seems peaceful, which is my original intention. The last thing that I want to do is create a situation where someone will get hurt, or a riot will take place, and then we can wind up with another Rodney King situation. That will most likely end peaceful demonstrations if it goes that far. Our constitution is being changed to accommodate our political thieves. It is easy for them to pass a law that limits the amount of people that can assemble or outlaw it all together. It has become common practice for a municipality to make a group of people purchase a permit to have a demonstration or a protest. Primarily it is for the revenue, but in the larger cities it is heavily enforced.

Myself, being a registered Democrat, have attended some local Democratic meetings, and I am surprised about how many voters are upset with the sitting president. They do not like the policies. They do not like the lies. They do not like the direction our country is going. They do not like the gang style tactics the party is using. And most of all, they do not like being called names when they confront politicians during town hall meetings. It makes them feel as if they are wasting their time. It just really pisses them off. The same sentiments are coming from the Republican side also. It appears that both parties agree on many things but the abuse of power continues daily. Now the town hall meetings have stopped. We are told that they are a waste of time for a politician to hold a town hall meeting when the voters disagree and disrupt the meetings. I may be wrong, but I think this is democracy. Our leaders try to mislead us by saying the anger expressed across to the rest of the country is not real, and these people are not sincere but are planted protestors. This tactic by the Democratic Party is in my favor for my idea.

In order to be talking to people about an assembly, I have to come up with a reason to have a march that will not bother the Congress and all the leaders. It has to be a non-threatening project that will not give the government a reason to feel threatened. In doing so it will seem peaceful. A peaceful assembly will limit the amount of security, and the less security, then the chance of someone getting hurt will be limited. But what will be a good reason for a large-scale march? That is going to require some intelligent thinking.

The reason for a large assembly is either a protest or a celebration. Naturally a protest march will require more security than a large-scale celebration. It wasn't until a news broadcast announced that our President is not only going to have the lighting of the Christmas tree at the White House, which has went on for decades, but this year he is going to let the other religions place their appropriate religious scenes at the White House and Lincoln memorial, so no one will be offended. Offended people do not vote for the ones that offend them. That seems to be a good place to gather a large amount of people with limited scrutiny.

It is one thing to have a million people go and watch the lighting of a Christmas tree at our Capitol, but having them participate in an overthrow of the government is a totally different thing. This is going to be the hard part of the mission, and keeping it quiet is going to be even harder. I really think that it is impossible. A coup at Christmas time does not seem to be a thing that we want to do for our children to remember. I have to come up with another plan.

The first thing is to go and talk with some of the people I know that have expressed their desire to change our present situation. I approach them with the idea that it is just a thought to get their opinion. To my surprise more and more people are thinking the same as I am. I even have a couple of my rich clients tell me that if I get something organized like that, they will help fund whatever I need. But this is just some people that I personally know. I believe that a total of two million people will be required to pull this off, and I am a little short on the count.

Knowing that we have to deal with the federal people, we have the states to consider and what involvement they will have will be important. I do not want the governors to activate the National Guard units in their states. So this takes on an additional planning stage. We do not have to take over each state capitol but we need to control them. I have to figure out a way where the governors will not let their guard units leave the state to help with the prevention of the takeover. Many are gone on deployment to the different wars that are going on, but we still have a large presence of National Guard that is not on duty. I do not want the Guard involved because the more of a military presence then the chance for someone getting hurt or killed will be greater than before.

I know a man that owns a gun shop locally that has been known to participate in some of the vast little militias that are scattered around Florida. He is a very vocal man about the government and criticizes them very openly. He once mentioned to me that it was time to have a revolution and kick the crooks out of Washington. He is easy to talk with and the subject at hand can be discussed with him without worry that he will inform anyone in an official capacity. He is struggling with his business because of all the new government regulations that involve gun and ammunition sales. However he is selling bows and crossbows as fast as he can get them in. Arrows are not being regulated like bullets.

After a lot of soul searching, I think I will see how far I can go without causing a problem or upsetting too many people. I wait for Jim, the gun shop owner, to show up this morning. It so happens that he has watched the morning news shows before he come to work today, and the news of the day has gotten him in a bad mood. This is a perfect time for me to toss the idea into the pot and see what he thinks.

As I enter his store he starts telling me what is being reported this morning on the news. It is more talk about making stiffer gun control laws that will limit his income and require him to do a terrible amount of additional paperwork per transaction. He is not happy, so this seems to be the perfect time to toss it out in the open and get his response.

I look at him and say, "Jim, why don't we just take over the government and put people in office that care about all of us little people? It won't be so hard. We just form million man march to Washington, do it armed, and with that many armed people no one will fire a shot. At least not any person with any form of a brain." He looks at me, and that is all it takes. He blurts, "We need to, and we need to do it now, and run those crooked sons of bitches out, and hang them to a tree. Better yet it would be good to take them over to Guantanamo Bay and let them rot in the hot sun."

I look at him and say, "Listen to me Jim. This is an idea, but you tell me what you think." I fill him in with all my little ideas and how and when to get people to show up in Washington. He has thought of this also and actually has a better idea. He says, "No, I have a better idea. We have Civil War re-enactments planned for the end of November around Fredericksburg, Virginia. At the same time another one will be going on at George Mason University right outside of D.C. I agree that I do not want to have our kids remember Christmas with a revolution instead of a time for fun and peace."

Jim walks over to the phone and dials a number. He says, "Henry can you come over to the shop? I got another guy here talking about what we did last weekend. Okay, I will see you in half an hour." Jim got a very serious look on his face and turns to me and says, "Security is our worst enemy. We need a lot of people to pull this off but only one with a big mouth can ruin it for all of us." I reply, "Why don't we announce our intentions to the media?" He looks at me like I am out of my mind.

I say, "No, we can leak information that people are confusing the re-enactment parade with a takeover of our government." The theme for the parade is the Union soldiers marching to the White House and the Confederate soldiers following in recognition of loosing the Civil War. I continue, "We can make a big deal out of the march and if someone says anything they will not take it seriously. We can say that the plans are to have a big parade going through Washington D.C., and a few stupid people are unable to separate fact from fiction." I figure the biggest problem is going to get people to go along with the idea and participate. Jim believes that it will be no problem at all. He has people that are wealthy, that have talked with him about this very issue. I was really amazed at the amount of people that have the same thought that we have.

We talked for half and hour or so, and then this big man with a ponytail wearing a confederate flag shirt, enters. He is the president of local people that re-enact different battles that occurred during the Civil War. He is a staunch survivalist and definitely anti-government. Jim tells me that he actually believes in a good government and laws, but Henry feels that the politicians are suppose to be a voice for the people the way our Constitution was set up, and not for their own agendas. So this issue we do agree with each other.

As Henry sticks his hand out for me to shake it he says, "I really believe that if we start shooting the liberal bastards one by one, many will leave office to save their ass. That will mean less work for us." I greet him and reply, "That will probably work but we will still have all of these bullshit laws on the books that we are dealing with now." He stood up straight and looks me in the eye and says, "Hell man you want to go after the whole enchilada don't you? I guess if we are going to do this then we might as well plan on doing it right. As far as all of these new laws we have , the new President just signs executive actions to do away with what he wants gone, and bypasses the Legislative Branch all together. You know the old saying, An executive order is nothing more than an instrument of dictatorship."

What I thought would be another problem is that our existing president attempted to establish a Civilian Militia. Our understanding was that it will be a copy of the Nazis' secret police under Hitler. It will consist of people who are sworn to protect the president. Henry said, "Hell, we already have people in that silly little organization, and we can put in place many more. I do not know how much help they will be, but at least we will have ears and eyes to inform us of any information leaking that we do not want out." The more inside information that we have will help us a great deal. It seems that some things are already in motion, and all that I am doing is forcing the issue to take place.

We arrange to meet at my house the next evening to go over some ideas and plans. Jim says that he has a couple of guys that I should meet that has ties to the groups that are going to put on the re-enactments in November. Come to find out, people from all over the United States routinely participate in these re-enactments and large crowds are normal. We need to come up with an idea to attract more people that will give the impression that the large amount of people will not become suspicious. The citizens of the southern states always wanted to control Washington, and this may be the time that they can do it.

More importantly than the actual act is, what happens after we achieved our initial goal? This is by far the most important aspect of the mission, and it has to be beneficial for the people to risk everything to participate in such an ordeal. The questions come up more rapidly than we have answers to. So each one of us will make a list of important things we think we need to be done in order to restore our government back to the way our founding fathers intended for it to be. We all understand that some things are outdated, but the basic concept of our Constitution is what we need to protect and restore. This idea is not a military coup d'etat, but the saving of our country. However the military does pose a small problem with our mission.

The next day Jim and Henry shows up and tells me that a few other people have flown in to hear what we have to say. I am somewhat worried because what we are discussing can be considered as treason. As they enter, I inform them that the discussions that we are about to have are purely hypothetical. Since I do not know these other men, I do not want to be set up for trying to overthrow the government and get thrown in jail myself.

One of the men is a retired judge from Indiana. He volunteered to be our legal adviser and has extensive knowledge of what we are talking about. He tells us of a plot decades earlier that involved a scheme to overthrow President Roosevelt. This plot was publicly revealed in 1934. It was commonly called the Plot Against FDR and also the White House Putsch. Wealthy businessmen organized this along with corporations that were going to incorporate the military to perform the task This is totally different than what we have in mind. Our intentions are to return our country back to the people the way it was intended. Our plan is to keep the military out of the situation, and do our best not to involve them but use them as allies. Having them on our side would be advantageous. The basic concept of the idea is the same. Many corporations are regulated so heavily that it is almost like being extorted. We still have organized crime, but this time our government has taken the role against businesses and is enforcing their plan of legalized extortion.

We have many things that apparently need to be done that I have not even thought of. Once we have achieved a takeover then security for the country is essential. That is where we can use our military to protect our infrastructure. We need someone inside our military to assure them that we are just forcibly re-electing lawmakers, and, within a couple of months a national election will be held within the country, but with a few different qualifications for lawmakers.

James Lucas, who is the retired judge, recommends that we give our organization a name that, will be non-threatening. We need to show that if the word get out, that it is totally a game of planning for a bunch of bored men and women. He says he can raise money from wealthy individuals that we can put into a bank account. We make a list of the best ideas, which can win prizes and trips to show participation in this planning game, in case the word gets out, and an investigation is initiated. Not only is this a great idea, but also we can actually advertise this game and while we will get great ideas from all kinds of people, they will not know the true intentions of the mission.

What James has done is inform us, with a very important piece of information. He tells us that he has issued warrants to law enforcement on people that had ONSTAR equipped vehicles. He says that even though the owner of the car does not subscribe to the services that ONSTAR provides, the government can still use the device to listen to conversations inside your car. So we are told to not discuss anything while in a General Motors car or one that was equipped with a system like ONSTAR. This is a very good piece of information, and this is why we like to get advice and ideas from everyone.

What we come up with is to do a small scale game, limiting the ideas that we need, and when we pick a winner we send out press releases, which in turn will create a larger amount of players. This way we can get military people, law enforcement, legal attorneys, militia personnel, reporters, and even past and current lawmakers. They all will think that it is a game, and the ultimate winner can win a million dollars for their idea. The initial presentation of a prize will make the game legitimate and will look as nothing more than a game. As we get more important people involved, they will gather some of their friends to submit more ideas. What we are after was the *greed* of money working in our favor. We get ideas that have had great attention paid to detail and the majority of them are things that we have not thought about. It turns out to be a great idea.

The idea of the game is simple. We came up with a country that could be the twin of America. It is called Atlantis, of all things. What we need from people is to plan the take over of the government of Atlantis. We put out in the planning stage that it is just like the United States as far as the military, the government branches, and economy of our country. This way it will be easy for players to think of ideas that we can use. It too suffers the same problems that we are facing. Basically, it is America, but is called Atlantis. Since Atlantis does not exist then all the players will simply relate to America and supply us with their ideas based on what they know. That is America. What started out as a few players at first, grew rapidly in players in just a couple of weeks. The name of the game was *Taking Back Atlantis*. The game gives people an out for their frustration and the players have no idea that they are supplying ideas for the actual takeover of America. We even have a Senator that is associated with the committee that oversees our security. It has taken off so fast that apparently no one suspects that it is going to be an actual event.

To get people interested we advertise that a new book is being put together on a government takeover. The best ideas will be used in the book, and the people who suggest ideas will be listed in the final print of the book. The game is the means to get good ideas for the book. But people want to get their name in print so bad that they often tell us things or give us ideas that they normally would not disclose.

The rules of the game are to come up with plans that will allow a takeover of Atlantis and the government. In order to win, a player will have to supply an idea or two on ways to accomplish the mission with a minimum of violence. The game concentrates on an individual to use their head instead of muscle. This is where people who have inside information about our military and security issues are so valuable. Again, greed is helping us get our information and ideas. Some people will provide us with information that is considered classified just to have the upper hand in their attempt to win the game. In order to get this information, all ideas are confidential and are rated on a scale. That is what we tell everyone, but almost every idea is checked out. This plan allows for an individual to supply us with information and not worry about their ideas becoming public. Some of the information that we get has to be classified. Other information was just great ideas. Sometimes it is good to get other views of the same basic idea. And we get plenty of information and views. All if this is in the name of *greed.*

Some of the ideas reflect the education of the player. Many of the ideas submitted are really stupid, showing the player has no education concerning our government or politics. Then we have some that make a point out of giving very detailed ideas. In some cases we are provided actual information on ways to do a certain task because they relate their ideas to America. That is the idea behind this game, to get people that have information that will be valuable to us in our mission. From the information we receive this will turn out to be more informative than we can ever imagine.

Second, James filed for a non-profit status for us with our intentions dedicated to the re-instatement of history in our government run schools. Our claim will make American history as well as political science mandatory. This is another attempt to make our organization look more legitimate. Education is always a good reason to either get non-profit status or to get a government grant.

We have a website that promotes the game and the future book. The response is staggering. The response is so great that we hired an IT guy to install our own server to handle all of the traffic. It appears that people do not have anything important to do in the evening, so they log on to our website and come up with ideas. We have almost become the new Twitter and Facebook, without the social input. It always amazes me how many times a simple idea can have such an important meaning to a plan. The ideas we acquire keep us running and researching to see how useful they can be. Very few ideas are useless or stupid. Although, there are some people that seem to have a circuit crossed in their pea brain. One idea is to steal a plane with a nuclear bomb and drop it on the capitol. I think this individual does not understand what we mean by non-violent. Our first goal is to secure our nuclear arsenal and not spread it around the country.

As the ideas come in along with donations, we have to get more people just to sort through all of the entries that we have received. It is not uncommon to have a hundred ideas pertaining to just one simple thing with a different view or plan of attack as I call them. Then the day comes that none of us expect. We actually received our certification as a non-profit organization. We are not after that status, but want to show that we are sincere in our intentions that are in the application for 501C(3) status as a non-profit corporation. James says he feels that we got that approval because he put on the application that none of the officers of the formed corporation is taking a salary. That shows we are sincere about what we are doing and not after money, so we solicit for donations and get a ton of money.

James submitted a request for a government grant. That is just so our organization will continue to look legitimate. When he wrote the grant, the majority of the requested money was to have these books printed on politics, economics, and history, and send them to the schools that have had their budgets cut so bad, they cannot afford to buy educational books. Three months after the grant was submitted, we received a two hundred fifty thousand dollar grant. What a surprise! The government has just supplied us with funds that are going to help overthrow their own establishment.

The American public is very open about how they feel about our present government, and is not afraid to express with us their feelings, but gives us some unusual and needed information. We get classified information from people who want to stay anonymous, but want that money for submitting the best idea. It turns out better than we actually thought. We even receive entries from politicians that go overboard in telling us how they can be run out of office, and are too stupid to realize that we may use this information to fulfill our mission. The politicians are so involved in making their personal situation better for them that they ignore and sometimes help us plan our mission.

Since our non-profit status, we are able to receive an old warehouse for free as long as we do improvements to bring it up to code and pay taxes and utilities on it. This is far above our dreams. We have contractors donate and perform repairs. Painters donate the paint and make the old building look like new. We are given furniture, computers, office supplies, floor coverings, a phone system, televisions, and even a couple used vehicles, for business use.

Then come some major cash donations. The people who donate, knows the real intentions, do not want their name used, so they bring us cash. We have a large vault that was constructed inside the building, and along with all the cash, we are able to hide weapons and donated ammunition that we receive. We also got an acre of land donated to us that has a small metal building on it. Underneath the small building is a hidden basement that was constructed many years ago, where we store the more important stuff that we don't want anyone to discover. The grant money that we receive from the government helps us maintain these properties.

As our membership grew in a very short time, we have expanded to many states and have gathered quite a bit of needed equipment and money. One of the re-enactment groups donated two old cannons that still work, and they have a few cannon balls. They have been able to purchase a large amount of black powder. One of our members who deal in surplus military equipment actually acquired a 105 mm Howitzer that is functional. He gave it too us but we have no rounds for the howitzer. A member in Colorado broke into a storage unit that contained a large number of 105 mm rounds, and screw in nose detonators, from a ski resort that uses them for avalanche control. We are on our way to becoming a well armed militia. But we stress often that the desired scenario is that we do not want one round of ammunition fired, and this operation is to be done very peacefully, using an overwhelming show of force. That is what we hope for, but when a large number of people are involved in something, things do get screwed up.

To show you how easy this is, because everyone is concentrating on his or her own problems and life, we put the Howitzer right outside our building as a display. No one ever suspects that it actually works and is going to be part of our takeover. Sometimes, the best ways of getting away with something is to do it in plain sight.

Our military members bring up situations with the nuclear weapons that our country has in inventory. We choose to let the Joint Chiefs of Staff have control over our nuclear armament, and if needed, they can use them to save American lives. We still need to figure out how we are going to inform the military that they will have control. But as with all things, eventually the idea would come to us. This may alarm people, but the one person that hates war more than the whiny war protestors is a General of a branch of military. The exception to the rule may have been George Patton, but the majority of our military knows that war is not a game and needs to be taken very seriously. They have seen what war is, and who better to put in control of the most dangerous weapons that we have. They will be in the hands of the people that will be in charge of launching such weapons. And it will take all of the Joint Chiefs approval before a weapon can be fired. One of the main reasons that we plan this in that way is to give the Pentagon a reason to believe in our efforts, and realize that we do not want to destroy our country, but save it. That idea of turning the nukes over to them will help in our efforts to continue, once the initial mission is completed. And besides, we most likely will never have the launch codes. And in reality trying to take over an installation that stores our nuclear arsenal will surely lead to many lives lost. The security at these places are the best that our country has in place it will be useless to even try.

The other thing concerning the military is the Generals are the experts on war. They will still be in charge of their appointed duties without the interference of civilians that know nothing about war and the security of a country. It will be critical as soon as the mission is over for the military leaders to contact our allies, and our enemies and let them know that the United States Military is fully operational, and in tact, and that during this changing of the guard, our patience will be very short. Our response to activities toward our people or country will be dealt with in the most severe action that we can place on a country or rogue organization. Our idea is that the Joint Chiefs can take control of the Guard and Reserve units temporarily, and start protecting our borders almost immediately, and that will keep them busy and out of our mission. This is what our hopes and plans are.

The example we came up with is that if our soldiers patrolling Baghdad come under attack from a particular area that has been a problem in the past, we will simply carpet bomb the location to were there will be no place to hide except for a pile of rocks and sand. The loss of civilian people will be unfortunate, but needed to protect our people. This will not take long before the residents of a certain area will make sure that this type of activity would not happen where they live. It is simply called "training our enemies".

Carpet bombing sounds very cruel in one respect, but since the United States seems to always go in and pay to repair damages that we do to a country during war, then it will be less expensive to start from scratch then to try and repair poorly constructed buildings. Third world countries are not stupid, and it will not take them long to understand their responsibility. For those that want help, we will help them if they asked for it. If they demonstrate they are unable to keep the terrorist out of their neighborhood, then we can assist them.

In the United States curfews will go into effect nation wide. These can be lifted depending on the area, and with the advice of the local authorities. Most importantly we have to get the confidence of the American people. A safer environment and extreme crackdown on crime will be one way to do this. Federal, state, and local law enforcement will not change, but just have new bosses. Violations such as looting, rape, murder, arson, destruction of property, and other severe violations, will be dealt with severe penalties. And if law enforcement feels threatened they will be ordered to shoot first and ask questions later. This will make sure that the curfews are abided by. For a temporary situation to aid in control our law enforcement, all demonstrations and protests will be outlawed without approval from our military experts. The National Guard units not protecting the border will aid law enforcement in their job, and will have full powers of the law to enforce the curfews and other needed laws. Naturally there will be some situations that will not be favorable with this idea. Overall it will be beneficial in the end.

To help secure our nation from illegal entry from our borders, our agents will be authorized to fire upon any individual that threatens them, without question. That also goes for landowners that have land bordering either Mexico or Canada. In order to get tough on smuggling and illegal immigration, extreme measures must be taken to secure our country from individuals that want to enter and do us harm. Word will travel fast, and it will limit these activities because the military will be patrolling the borders. A breach in security will be seen as an act of war and dealt with in that respect.

Under the new rules, until a new government takes over in our place, a smuggler will most likely get shot upon detection. All of these initial plans will have to be implemented and discussed, but it will only take a matter of minutes for a decision instead of the way that we used to deal with laws. Again our best security advisers will be our military leaders. During this planning we have several objectives. First, and foremost, is security for our country, and then our people. Second, is the daily routine of our people will not be disrupted, with the exception of the curfews. Setting a date for a new election will be announced, and the criteria of the individuals that will be qualified to run for office will be announced also.

A current lawmaker can be eligible to be nominated back as long as that individual never took any special interest money and agrees to go along with our plan. They will play a very important role as advisors since they have knowledge of the legislative branch. The objective of this operation will be to get rid of the greedy, selfish individuals, that care not for the citizens of the United States. We want to restore our government to the ways of the people, and not the individual aspirations of the elected officials by getting rich.

This is not unusual for us. We did this same action in Iraq but we will do it without the violence and destruction. We learned a great deal from taking over Iraq, and one of the things that no one expected was the large scale looting that went on. This is the reason for the curfews, and using the Guard to help maintain individual states. This gives them a purpose, and a reason to be out patrolling the streets of their area, and gives them the discretion to do whatever is needed to maintain law and order, and peace. In other words, the United States is going to be under martial law. The news media will also play a big role. They will report on the actions of our law enforcement controlling the curfews. Broadcasting the shooting of resisting looters and burglars will limit the activity of the criminals planning a large scale shopping spree on the American public. Since protest will be temporarily banned, the protests that we see when an individual of a different race is killed by law enforcement will be eliminated. In reality, forced action against protestors will most likely have to occur in order for them to realize that we are serious about maintaining the law during this transition. This will be a temporarily disruption of the freedom of speech, but will be necessary, and will have a limited time until we get a handle on new elections and the job of removing all of the Good Ole' Boys from Washington. Another way to limit the criminal activity and protests during this time is that a person on welfare will be required to report to a location picked by the municipality, that they live in on a daily basis, for a work program. There will be no more sitting at home watching the View or Oprah. If the people of the United States are going to pay someone for welfare, then they will earn that money by cleaning the streets or mowing the grass in the common public areas. The reason behind this thinking is that many people that attend protest have no job. That is why they have time to go out and bitch and destroy things. If a person works all day and is tired, the chance for them to stray out during curfews and attempt to destroy property will be limited. Many of them might loose some weight, which will be healthy for them in the long run.

As we sit down and toss in ideas and plans for our mission James just asks me, "What plans do you have? What do you want to gain by doing this dangerous thing? I look around the room and say, "Nothing for myself. I am tired of the way things are headed. I have no political desires, and I don't want anything out of this except that our government returns to the control of people. I want to see a government that has a passion to do the right things and make the right decisions. I have a group of grand children, and I would like them to live in a secure safe place, where they have a voice in what happens to them."

I look at James and ask him, "What do you want?" He says, "I want our courts to follow the law and not make it up as it goes. I want our courts to be an organization that deals with justice and not a facility to make money and destroy young lives. I want limits on terms that lawmakers can spend in office, and I want the pork to stop in our bills. That is nothing more than internal lobbying for hire." It is well known that our legislative branch will barter for what they want but they tax us on the practice of bartering. And, above all, we want to make lobbyist that give money to leaders, against the law, with severe penalties.

So far it appears that everyone involved in this planning stage has no personal desire to take a position in the government by the coup. But all, have legitimate reasons for participating and risking their future. Good ole' American values is what we all stand for. We do have a high-ranking retired Marine that has a desire to be high up in the Border Patrol Agency. That is fine with all of us, because if we pull this off, then the border will be closed down immediately after the take over.

It has been decided that we have to know our members of this particular group, and we have to know everyone. We decided that if we are going to make our country a democratic , and not a social state, we will compile lists of needed things to do, but vote on everything. We appoint James temporary chairman, and his duties are to run the show on the legislative side of this. This is the decision making part of our group as well as maintaining order and giving us legal views of the Constitution.

Bob who is the retired Marine, is in charge of security. He has an idea to make known that we have thousands of members. But with that membership size, if security was breached and talked about, we have to give the impression that it will be a matter of time before they will be eliminated. This is not true, but we have to make it look dismal for those who talk about our membership or plans. And for those that are informing authorities, their demise will be slow and very painful. The information will include that our members are law enforcement, FBI, U.S. Marshals, Secret Service, and the Justice Department. The reason for this is that anyone who is promised protection will know they cannot hide from our wrath. But the ultimate goal will be that no one will get hurt, other than his or her pride and income. And especially that no one will be killed. We will be more legitimate if we can pull this off without someone dying.

When you think about what I say about all the different people involved in security and law enforcement it is actually becoming a reality. It appears that many people know of someone that is a member of those agencies, but has the same feelings as we do. Or they have their own reasons for participating. Membership is growing, and money is coming in faster than we can count it. It has become not only a state wide organization with different charters, but also some people in foreign countries is donating money.

We have a Chinese man, that has become a United States citizen, that has mentioned our plans to a friend in China who has a great deal of wealth. He has offered us explosives instead of money. It was a quick vote of NO. The idea is to preserve our country, and not damage the infrastructure or anything else, except for removing people that are like slime and are far guiltier of more serious crimes than half of our population in our prisons. We want this to be remembered as *the shot that was never fired around the world.*

I am able to travel and attend other meetings that are small groups of people that do reenactments of the Civil War. We start by tossing around the idea of a coup, but act like we are not planning one to see the reaction of these people. I am absolutely floored by the amount of people that are for something along these lines of thinking. It is so easy in the southern states. Our theme song for us is by Charlie Daniels, "South's Gonna do it Again". But we make our intentions clear that this is to be good for all citizens, and not just residents of the southern states. We will work hard to recognize different state cultures with the exception of California. That state is so full of wacky, strange, and dangerous minded crooks, that we will have to change some things concerning that state for the betterment of our country.

We approach the Civil War enthusiast like we are promoting the game. We have to do this because some areas supply law enforcement for security, whether we want it or not. We will approach one individual that we feel we can trust, and will rely on him, or her, to point out ones that we can trust. Then they will give us other people that they know and they can trust. Sounds very difficult, but in reality, it is very easy. We have a committee that sends at least one individual to every meeting the Civil War enthusiast have. The reason is to listen to the members of their organizations, and to scope out people that we will be able to trust. More importantly, is to spot those members that we can not trust. It is imperative that we get as much information about different security measures that each individual state has. A requirement is that our people will take many pictures. We want to see who is there, and if any of them attend multiple meetings.

The initial plans for the states are that some may be overrun. Most of them will not know what happened until it is over. We are working on securing all Army Reserve Units and National Guard Units. You secure their building, which will contain weapons and special communication equipment, and if they cannot get to them, then they cannot use them against us. This will require a lot of people. The plan is that all funds from the federal level to the states will halt until they are also on board with the re-instatement of our Constitution. Once we get to talk with them, they will be forced to come on board. The majority of people will support this type of change once people they trust explain the idea to them.

We do not use computers at all except for research so there are no electronic notes except for the game ideas. Our actual plans are written down in one binder and it is hidden from everyone other than our little group. If for some reason our computers are seized, then they will contain only game details and information about our non-profit organization. All legal with nothing that looks dangerous to our country. We expect that some day we may have problems with law enforcement, and count on our building to be searched as well as our personal residences. Emails are restricted to not include any plan information. We have pre-programmed hard drives for each computer that can be installed in a matter of minutes. This also will add a layer of protection in case some member has a bad piece of information on their computer. We have to make sure the computers are clean and our group appears to be operating at very high standards. Sometimes the latter is hard because some of our members seem to be raised in a nut house.

To be totally in the open, our envelopes that we send out to people actually has a small paragraph on the front asking them to contact us and ask about the game, because they can be the next big prize winner. We want it to be seen so many times by officials, that they just ignore them after a while. We are a charity begging for money from people just like a politician. It works for them, so it will work for us. What also helps us is that we had thousands of books printed for schools, and when we deliver them, we make sure it is a major event with lots of positive publicity. This makes us more legitimate and most of us enjoy doing this for our kids.

We have a few members that send in their ideas concerning the game who reside in Washington, D.C. They do it as a group, which is acceptable for us. We like ideas from groups because they have done the big part of the discussion and decision making for us. The information they provide to us for their plan is extremely important. There are members of the military, and I do not mean everyday soldiers, but members of the military in high-ranking positions. Some work at the Pentagon and the White House. They too want to win some extra legal money and are very generous with their ideas. We have heard that occasionally you can walk down the halls of the White House and hear someone talking about playing the game. The White House staffers and employees think because of their positions that they will have an edge over the rest of the population.

Our Washington boy's plan is to totally shut down Washington, D.C. There will be roadblocks set up at every entrance, and we will control who was coming and going. It will be unfortunate to residents of Washington, but that will also put a halt to all the crime that occurs in the city of our Capitol. The local police will be in charge of taking care of the criminal element, and this will be on the list of essential things to take care of. and this will rid our Capitol of the extreme crime it has at whatever cost. Political correctness, profiling, and any other means that we will use to complete our mission, is not out of reason. This will be the only place where lives may be endangered and lost. The criminal element will either get out, give up, or be eliminated.

It will be made public, and enforced. I am sure that the NAACP is going to have a field day filing court motions, but they will all be declined by executive order.

We all know that Capitol Hill will not be a tremendous challenge, but the White House is a different story. The Pentagon is not going to be a problem because we are going to deal with the ranking military men, and they will have no involvement at all with the coup except to implement orders on the current wars and security of our borders. That task is what they are required to do by their job descriptions, and we are not going to interfere in that. Actually we think that many will be on board with us because they resent civilian interference in their planning and operations on military matters. We feel that they can do a better job without our input, and we will have more loyalty when they see that we are not making America a dictatorship but returning it back the way it is suppose to be. Unfortunately, they have to be reminded that they too will face severe penalties for failure to do their job as directed. We plan on asking them to pick someone that could act in the capacity of Secretary of Defense, but with a different role. Instead of being a messenger for the President on what he wants the military to do, he would be involved in coordination and planning. This will all up to a vote between the Commanders. It will also be his or her job to make sure funds, and needed equipment, will be available for any missions that the military needs to perform. The Secretary of Defense will be a one-man security committee that can order anything that the military needs without fear of funding or use. To help with our mission on gaining support from our countrymen is to order a large stockpile of weapons that we use regularly in military action. This not only will make us stronger but will help the economy by manufacturing weapons.

At one meeting we had in Alexandria, Virginia, an 82-year-old man came up to me and asked me if we are planning a coup and a takeover of the White House. He said he was in favor of our actions because he felt we are truly concerned with returning our country back the way it was, and he feels we can re-instate the pride that America once had. He tells us that he has the detailed plans of the escape routes and secret tunnels from the White House and Capitol Hill. We have heard of these legends before, but we have never seen actual plans of tunnels or escape routes underground.

One of our people that is in our security group asks him, "If these tunnels actually exists they will surely be alarmed and very secure will they not?" He says, "They damn sure are but only the ones that are currently opened, but not the original ones that some wall has been built in front of the access." I looked at him and say, "I would like to see those plans as well as anything that you have on these tunnels." He nods his head and turns and walks off. I feel that the information that he claims he has is not factual.

It is three days later when I receive a phone call from the old man and he tells me that he has the plans and information that I need. I cannot believe it. He agrees to meet us in front of the White House to take possession of his information. While looking through the fence at the front of the White House he appears next to James, who went to meet him.. He says, "I have been here hundreds of times and it always makes my heart skip a beat. This is a very sacred place for me and I want to remember it as a good place, that helps, but does not limit, the people of this country." He hands James the plans and descriptions of things and says, "You look at these for a couple of days and when you are ready call me at this number." He hands James a business card with only his phone number and walks away. I was anxious to see what he has and if it can help us at all. Only a very small percentage of information is valuable in our endeavor, but we have to look at it all. The White House is our most complicated problem to this whole mission.

James and I took them home and spread them out on my dining room table. I am amazed that they have the initial tunnels, the revised tunnels, and finally the remaining tunnels that are under surveillance by the Secret Service and White House security. Even a fire truck, that can always be seen on the news when the President gets out of his helicopter is parked intentionally over a grate the covers one of the escape routes. We learn that the fire truck was being used to cover the entrance against bad weather as well as being available in case of a fire. What is amazing is that the unsecured tunnels have detailed plans and explanations telling us how the openings are covered, and with what material, and the thickness of the closure. I am only concerned if this is accurate, and has not been revised again since these prints were done. He assures us that they are accurate because his friend still works there, and will always tell him when they do something to change things below the White House.

Jim and I have discussed the White House many times. We feel that it is a symbol, more than a place, that ran the country. The symbol cannot be damaged because it belongs to the people of this great country. We are going to the trouble of planning on taking over the White House, but we really prefer that no one enters that building. But we will do what ever it takes to make sure that the current administration never sets foot in there again. We have talked with people that retired from the military, that are familiar with the Air Force, and the fleet of military planes that the President uses. At the time of the operation, we have to seize control of those planes if for no other reason than their communication equipment. We met a member of the Air Force that is very interested in our game. He seems convinced that it is more than a game. At first we are concerned with him. One night he made a statement. He says, "If this is really going to happen here in the United States, then I can make the problem with the secured aircraft a non-issue." He tells us that a simple order via a secured Internet connection can render all of the executive airplanes grounded. He even says that he can get the planes recalled no matter where they are, or who is being transported. It is a security issue that is built in to protect the planes from being taken over or when ever there is a significant threat against them. The communication equipment on the plane is also a matter of national security.

James has a contact that believes a retired general from the military might be in the mood to join our little organization. During the Gulf War he was forced out and made to retire over a decision he made that was not popular with the president that was in office at that time. He is a true dedicated American that believes in the Constitution and is a scholar of many of the past presidents. Within the military organizations he is regarded as a patriot and is well respected by all. Timing on approaching him is the problem that we have. He will be a big benefit for us because of the respect he has within the military community. Other information that he can provide us with is secret bases that can be used by government and military personnel in case of an emergency. We need to know about all of these secured areas and make a plan to secure them.

We decided that in order to force the individual states to conform to our plan of action, they will immediately be cut off from all federal funds until they provide a detailed plan of action for them to reform their laws and policies, to go along with the new ones that will be implemented. The policy of no more money to officials will still be a felony with a very high penalty if violated. Individuals caught and found guilty in a military court, since we will be under martial law, would be severe and quick with a minimum of 25 years per violation for taking illegal contributions and gifts. And they will not go to a country club prison but to general population in a federal penitentiary.

But that still leaves the Guard and Reserve units that are in the different states. James tells us that his friend, the General, will research that situation and come up with an idea. It is a belief that with his help we can actually have allies in the Pentagon that will help us with our endeavor. We will also have to deal with all of the local and state law enforcement agencies. We will have to have envoys that can contact the governors of each state. We have to come up with a plan to make it acceptable for each state to go along with our situation. We need some good people that are well respected throughout the United States, that are credible. We have to come up with a plan that will benefit the states to stay out of what we are doing. Our problem will not be the citizens of each state, but the officials. This is going to require more thought and planning. It will be absolutely essential that we lock down Washington D.C. to keep people out while we are doing our mission. And the most important part of what we are going to do, will be to have control, or at least partner, with our military.

Since our economy is in a terrible mess, and all of the states are hurting financially also, money seems to be the answer to most of our problem. Our present government is giving money away to foreign countries like it is candy. One of our member's think that the best plan of action is to stop all outside money transfers, and give it to the states that will cooperate with this transition. We are pumping billions of dollars to terrorist organizations and countries. It is time to stop that, and let them know that they are on their own for a while until our new government is set up. If we have any trouble from any of them we simply will remind them that we have control of our nuclear arsenal, and it will not be in their best interest to piss us off. The easy way to deal with terrorism is to eliminate the terrorist. Those people that comply with our request will be rewarded in the future, but those that do not will cease to exist. After all, one of the main reasons for doing what we are doing is to secure the United States from all threats. It is time to stop paying extortion money and just deal with the problem.

During our discussions with planners and military people, it is clear that at some point we may have to deal with a possible breach of our security. The borders will not present those problems because they will be dealt with swiftly, and in a harsh manner, to curb the flow of people, weapons, and drugs that are coming across our border. Zero tolerance will take care of that fairly fast. After all, those crossing the borders are considered invaders and smugglers. If a certain drug cartel gives us a lot of problems, then we will send a couple of planes into Mexico and take care of them on a personal basis. Our goal is that the citizens of our country will not be harmed, but outsiders will be open to very aggressive penalties. The Mexican government will be no problem because we buy nearly all of their oil, and stopping that will persuade them to follow our procedures or starve to death.

The other agencies that will have to stay running will be the Treasury Department, the Justice Department, naturally the CIA, and FBI. Deals are being made with some private firms that provide security details for hire. You know we started calling them contractors, but actually they are mercenaries. Some of the best military people that we train will be utilized because the present administration and Congress outlawed them from being used in our conflicts. That forced a lot of them seek employment with other countries, and sometimes their missions are against the United States. They are willing to participate with our mission, and again protect the interest of their country.

Most are loyal Americans, but they too have to feed their families and pay their mortgages.

A couple of our members who are in the banking business came up with one of the best ideas to help secure the trust of the American people, as well as the other countries. We will have to manipulate the stock market. With an increase in the stock market, even slightly after the take over, the American people will relax more than if it crashed again. We can announce that we will be putting the banking, industrial, and manufacturing businesses back in private hands. They have been in control of the government since 2009, and things are not doing that well. A small but steady rise in the stock market will build confidence. In order to do this we most likely will have to control the stock exchange, but when the investors see a positive and not a negative decline in their investments, business should resume to normal and maybe improve. We have formed a small committee to deal with that situation and let us know what we will need to do to accomplish that mission. We have turned into a greedy nation, and with money values increasing it will make most people happy. As we have learned in the past ten years, as long as the public is making money, they ignore everything else that is going on around them.

Our First Amendment has turned into a joke, and to pull this off right, we will have to control the press. Or, at least, we will have to control the information that they receive. We can establish our own little press corp. You know that the reporters will die to get a position on this assignment. We will have to manipulate them as well. The ones that get out of line can report first hand on how water boarding feels. The press will be useful to show that our government is still running, and is headed toward a better situation than it has been in for many years. All federal lawmakers will have to be secluded from the public for a time. What we do not need is to have the normal news panels debating situations and making the public nervous. Taking over some of the television and radio stations will have to be part of our plan. We can simply make them re-apply for a license before they can broadcast, and limit what they report. In reality we have to have state run television and radio for a while. I really hate to see that happen, but it seems like the only way to keep a calm presence on the public.

Then one of our members came up with this idea. Why not get one of our previous presidents or vice-presidents to be a figurehead, so to speak, to make the country feel more relaxed. If not one of them then a respected high ranking official that we have seen daily on the news and have respect for. If we can convince such an individual to help us after the take over is done, then our job will be so much easier. The public will be relieved that someone that has experience is in the front seat at the wheel, so to speak, but actually they will only be a person that is speaking to them. Past presidents may not be totally admired, but at least having an experienced person on television will relieve tension. We have an idea of a man, that at the end of his presidency, was not totally popular, but is saddened by what our country has turned in to. The one point that everyone agrees with about this individual is he did protect our country, and after an initial attack, there were no more on our soil. But this time the military does not need to get permission to protect our country from the President or the Congress. They have Carte Blanc to go after the bad guys even before something happens. Pro-active policing is what we call it.

CHAPTER 4

▼

THE PLAN IS COMING TOGETHER

It is time to start making some final plans. During our talks with other people we were able to get some of the oil companies to come on board with us. All we had to do was to promise to lift the ban on oil refineries so they can build and expand some of their existing gas manufacturing plants. The regulations that are being imposed on them have hurt the industry. They are limited in the amount of profit they can make. Before the government would take the excess in a new tax that was imposed. Again greed aided us. All that we ask is that fuel will stop when we take over until we get control of our government. The only fuel that will be delivered will be to our military. This will shut the airlines down as well as public and private transportation. State and local law enforcement will get shipments of fuel, if they participate willingly with us.

With the State of New York imposing new and harsh taxes on the rich, many of them have come on board with us for revenge. New York has lost some of the largest taxpayers they have, and are begging them back. It is too late. It helps us because the wealthy is angry and they choose to give us help and money instead of the state government. These individuals also brought us many wealthy people from other states. One of the largest real estate tycoons that New York has is one of our biggest supporters. A prominent talk show host is one of the first to leave New York and has agreed to spread the word after the take over to help calm people down. He will be one of only three people that will be broadcasting after we complete our mission. That is until things settled down and we lift the media blackout. We have no idea on how long the blackout will last.

We have gained a large membership from our military. Our current President has stopped our missile defense program, which scares the majority of our public, as well as many of our military. We are totally defenseless against an incoming missile from a hostile country. It will not be very long before the United States will be defenseless toward an invading enemy. This action by the current administration allows us to gain some members that are in some of our most secure military agencies. The military people know that it is a matter of time before we get attacked. The fear is that we will be hurt and hurt badly. It is the belief from within our military that our President is actually trying to get America taken over by a foreign country so that he can become the sole dictator. Socialism is just a stepping-stone to get what he wants. Our plan is to stop that before he can accomplish his goal.

In the past few months we have assembled some of the highest ranking members of the military, the best people known to handle the economy, some of the wealthiest, and most influential people in America and abroad. We have college educators that are experts on politics and the Constitution. We have almost every member of the medical community as well as many large pharmaceutical companies. The majority of the private contractors that perform security are on our side. We have a segment of people from almost every sector and occupation from the United States, except for the entertainment industry. Many of them have turned so liberal that it makes many of us sick to our stomach. In reality we are dealing with real life circumstances and we have no interest in the movie business.

It is being reported to us by our membership that everything needed to shut down Washington D.C. is in place and waiting. The re-enactments are scheduled to start in a few days. An order from our government has been issued to add additional security features to all of our guard and reserve units. No one officially knows of this order but all of the unit commanders were sent orders to comply with security companies to upgrade their security features. No one objects to this. In reality a device will be added to all of the buildings that will make their security alarms inactive via a radio signal. When the appropriate time is near the alarms can be shut down and entrance can be made into these properties without causing any concern. The objective of this is to secure, or take any and all weapons. Without weapons, no one can fight. We have received information that someone from every reserve and guard unit across the country is in our membership and will aid us in this process of our mission. Many of the units are deployed overseas. Many left their weapons and received new ones in the war zone. These weapons will be secure in a safe place so that no one could get a hold of them. Specialized weapons that we might need, as a show of force, have been shipped on trucks to us to various locations. The majority of the Guard units will not even be entered but will have military guards guarding the facilities. The signs posted outside of the buildings simply state that the unit is under the control of the Pentagon and lethal force is authorized for trespassers.

The trucking companies are willing participants in our mission. They are no longer making money by shipping supplies across our country, because of new regulations imposed and rising fuel prices. The government has almost put them out of business. We have private trucks both sitting and waiting for orders, and trucks on their way to predetermined destinations. There are hundreds of trucks being used, and many of them are hauling food, water, and personal items to the area. Feeding a couple of million people is no small chore.

One of the major airlines is participating also. The CEO of that company is a strong participator in our organization. He has arranged for us to get some major donations of equipment and money from some of his business associates. There are planes scheduled to be in certain airports to help us transport members essential to the coup. They are classified as charters so that they do not arouse suspicion. Also loading will not be done through the airport. It will be done at hangers so that no one can see who is departing but also no security checks. This allows weapons to be transported as well. The planes are scheduled to land at Ronald Reagan National Airport, Dulles International, and Thurgood Marshall International Airport. This is a plan that was set up by one of our members' that is high up in the Federal Aviation Administration. Every airport official has been told that the arriving planes from this airline will be performing a mission of national security, and is to be escorted to a hanger. The luggage and cargo will be loaded in cargo trucks and the people will be loaded on buses. Private security vehicles will be supplied by the airline to make it look official, but will not make it look suspicious. We have thirty-two planes that are scheduled to assist us. Charter busses from all over the country have been chartered to carry people to Washington D.C. We have the departures and arrivals spread out over four days. We can bring in a lot of people in four days. They are coming from every state in the nation. Constant arrivals twenty-four hours a day are not uncommon. This plan gives us time to deal with the arriving members, and do it in a relaxed manner. We do not want a real large group of people to be noticed arriving like a herd of cattle. A steady stream of arriving tourists and business people is quite common in and around the city.

At predetermined locations, that are going to be used in the Civil War Reenactments, portable toilets and showers are being set up. Plans for these were made months in advance. The suppliers of the toilets did not ask any questions about the quantity of facilities we requested. They are just happy to get the business. We gave them a very substantial down payment. They are quite pleased to assist us.

One of our plans is to use as many local places to purchase some of the supplies that we need. Instead of trucking them in we have the local merchants deliver our supplies. There were no questions. Everyone is pleased to get a large order of merchandise. A farm that raises chickens for laying eggs was contracted a couple of months before our arrival. They had to add a large quantity of laying hens to their facility to get enough eggs we requested. We initially ordered over two hundred thousand dozens eggs. Refrigerated trucks full of meat and other food are on their way to Washington D.C. Portable kitchens are being shipped along with the supplies needed to sustain a food facility.

When I witness the enormous venture that we have organized it totally amazes me. We are extremely fortunate to have a retired purchasing agent from Wal-Mart. Ordering the required products is just another day at the office for this guy. Whenever the upper members met and we talked about something we needed, he always knows what is needed to compliment our requirements. His planning abilities are far superior to what any of the members had ever seen before. He is like a walking, talking, computer. There will be a place in the new government for him.

We have a large tent that is at one of our campsites that we plan on using as a medical tent. Whenever a large population of people is associated together, someone always gets sick. The different bacteria in the local water, as well as the environment, always make the people with weak immune systems ill. Another surprising event is that when our member doctors came to set up shop, they brought some of their associates. We have surgeons, dentist, general practitioners, orthopedic surgeons, various nurses, and almost a specialist in every field of medicine. There is even a Veterinarian that brought his specialized X-Ray equipment that he uses on racehorses. Computerized X-Rays appear on a computer screen seconds after they are taken. Some of the doctors could not believe the equipment that he had because many hospitals were still using film for regular X-Rays.

Since every plan that we have come up with is in action it is time that the leaders of our group travel to our Capitol. Many of us have never been to Washington D.C. We took off in one of our chartered jets from Gainesville, Florida. There is thirty-six of us. We are booked in a hotel in Frederick, Maryland. It is a few miles from the area where most of our members are, but is far enough from Washington to stay out of sight. From there we set up a network of communication equipment via the Internet. We booked the entire hotel for the other members that are essential to our operation. We have access to huge conference rooms where we can have our private meetings. We booked the conference rooms as a company reunion for a major security company. We told the management of the hotel that we were going over information on work that was done overseas for our government. The information we explained to them was classified, therefore we require their people to only come around when requested. Our request will be honored.

When we got to Frederick, Maryland we landed at the Municipal airport there. It is barely big enough to handle our jet. The airport does have a 5000' runway and according to the pilot, he could land the plane and have room to spare. We all hope he is right. When we did land, there was a very nice bus waiting for us. Frederick is the home of the Monocacy Civil War Battlefield and the National Museum of Civil War Medicine. There is history in this town and it will soon be part of more history. When we arrived the rest of our members, that are part of planning and operations, greeted us. We all went to a meeting room and got all of our little chitchat done before we got serious. For many of us there are a lot of new faces that some of us never have seen. I stood and looked around and thought, man we all would look funny in prison garb. In reality there has been more planning and actions by our committees than I realized, and have knowledge of. I seem to be just floating around in my own little world while other more qualified people handled the planning stages.

As I look around the room I am totally amazed. I see people that I have seen in the news. I also see a military General. He is retired and he is wearing civilian clothes, but he has a face the whole country knows. As people are moving around the room attempting to find a seat, I could have sworn that I saw the Chief Justice of the Supreme Court. When I lost him in the crowd, I began to look around. At this time James yelled at me to come over and meet some people. As I walk over to where James is I keep searching for the person that looks like the Chief Justice. I cannot find him so I just figure my tired eyes are playing tricks on me.

I mingled around for about twenty minutes when James decided to get the meeting started. Someone dimmed the lights and turned on an overhead projector. The beginning is a programmed slide show. The first picture is a picture of Old Glory blowing in the wind. The other pictures are of the White House, the Capitol, the Pentagon, the Statue of Liberty, as well as many more from around the United States. Then the Constitution of the United States is shown and that is where the slide show stops. With the picture of our Constitution displayed on a large screen, James welcomes everyone.

The conference room is secure so that no one will be listening to our meeting. James introduced the people that are involved, and then he pointed to me and said, "For those of you that are wondering how you got into this crazy scheme, I would like you to meet Steve Taylor. Steve thought of this mission, like many of us have. He just nudged it some and the ball started rolling. And a few short months later here we are." James pointed around the room and introduced several other people and then the planning of the final stages of our operation was set in motion. The room contained some of the wealthiest people in the world. We are a mixed crowd. We have businessmen, military men, and politicians from all levels of corruption, loyal Americans that want real change, and some of the best planners in the country. Amazingly we all came together to work on one goal. That goal is to take America back to the days where we lived by the Constitution. So many Americans have died while defending the basic idea of freedom and real democracy. Even though we are not sure how this operation is going to turn out, we are proud to be associated with the mission and the people.

After the initial introduction of people, James called on people that are handling different phases and parts of the operation. The individual that deals with recruitment and membership for the mission, as well as the game, stood up and informed us that we have over six million volunteers willing to participate. Between the game and the money that our non-profit group has brought in is over fifty million dollars. That figure does not include private donations from major contributors. I never asked how much money we have. If we needed funds for some activity, I simply would ask if we have enough to finance whatever I was dealing with. I always got the answer, "Yeah, we can handle that." I was unaware the operation was doing so well. This amount of money showed me that support was better than I thought.

One of our members claimed to be related to George Ross. Ross was one of the original signers of the Declaration of Independence. They are from Pennsylvania. Vincent Ross came up front to the table where James was and spoke. He said, "For those of you that have any reservations about what we are planning on doing here in a few days, let me put something on the projector for you to read. This is from our Declaration of Independence." On the screen appeared our Declaration of Independence. A portion of a paragraph was highlighted and it says, "That whenever any Form of Government becomes destructive of these ends, it is the Right of the People to alter or to abolish it, and to institute new Government laying its foundation on such principles and organizing its powers in such form, as to them shall seem most likely to effect their safety and happiness. Prudence, indeed, will dictate that Governments long established should not be changed for light and transient causes; and accordingly all experience hath shewn that mankind are more disposed to suffer, while evils are sufferable than to right themselves by abolishing the forms to which they are accustomed. But when a long train of abuses and usurpations, pursuing invariably the same Object evinces a design to reduce them under absolute Despotism, it is their right, it is their duty, to throw off such Government, and to provide new Guards for their future security."

Vincent read that passage with everyone following along. He paused for a few seconds and said, "You see folks. We are doing exactly what our forefathers laid out. The problems that we are having are not light and transient. They are very serious and if we do nothing, our country will never return to the great nation that it once was. If we do nothing then we will be worse off then if we continued to be under the rule of Great Britain. Our country has evolved into the best place to live until a few years ago. We are under a Socialist regime and our present government is doing its best to convert our democracy into a dictatorship. With that thought I cannot, and will not, be a part of being told what I can do, and when I can do it, under the rule of a selfish and dangerous dictator." He walked off and received a standing ovation. Standing there, one could just feel the electricity in the air. It was like a shot of B-12. Vincent stated that in our information we will put out to the press will include this passage for all to hear. Many of our younger citizens are so poorly educated, they do not know what is in the Declaration of Independence.

Our next person to speak is one of the men on a committee that deals with the Treasury Department and the current financial activity of America. He has a proposal that he wants to toss around and get ideas on. His proposal is a way to control the stock market without manipulation that is not factual. Previous administrations of our government have thrown trillions of dollars into the economy to get it stimulated. Every time they do, then the stock market drops. When the stock market drops, the citizens panic. His proposal is to put the money in the stock market. Secretly buying stock will advance the value and will show a rise in trading. It is factual that we will have to put more money into the economy, but this seems like the best way to do it to gain the trust of the population. Our people will see a consistent value, or an increase in stock value, and this will make them feel relaxed. With the stock prices increasing, investors will jump on board and start buying additional stocks. When it starts to increase consistently, more people will buy, and they will reap the rewards of the rising prices. This manipulation will cost the taxpayers less money in the end than a plan that for years threw money at a problem, and does nothing to correct it. If we do not get control of our economy, we will be headed for bankruptcy. A Great Depression the world has never seen before. As he explained his idea he asked, "So what do you think?"

As our best financial wizards talk amongst themselves, the room sounded like a bunch of busy bees. I look across the room, I see people writing and figuring. Calculators are being used in such a fashion that some of them start smoking. The enthusiasm in the room is phenomenal. Then one of the members who is most likely the largest real estate developer in the country stood up and said, "This will work. This will work and cost us less, than any other plan that we have tried. I cannot believe that we did not do this in the first place." I am not a big financial wizard but to see these tycoons get so excited is like nothing I have ever seen before. The great part of this idea is we do not have to lie to the American public, but we will not tell them the United States Treasury will buy stock at a surprising rate. The members involved in the stock market agree that the idea will work and the money that we invest will not only multiply but will help in lowering our current deficit. This plan will help jump-start some of the businesses that are being hurt by the economy. James called for a short recess so people can stretch their legs. Surprisingly they all stayed in the room for a good while talking about this great plan.

I notified the hotel that they can serve dinner and most everyone went to the bar they provided for us to have a drink. We have to constantly go around and remind people to be careful what they are saying so the help at the hotel will not over hear them. But emotions are high.

We broke for an hour and a half and then we all came back into the room to continue with our talks. This time our speaker does not have the best news of the day. A couple of days ago, one of our private freighter ships was high jacked by pirates in international waters, off of the coast of Somalia. A total of thirty-six Americans are on board. The news media has not reported much on this situation. Our speaker was a high-ranking officer from the United States Navy. The Navy dispatched a number of ships to the area, and when they arrived, and was in the proximity of the captured ship and the pirate mother ship, word came down from the White House to not get involved. The administration did not want to upset any foreign country that may be funding the pirates. Because of that decision the members of our Navy watched as the pirates executed many of the sailors, and waved to our Navy as they threw the bodies overboard. Luckily one of the sailors on one of the destroyers filmed what was going on and sent it to a news organization. The whole country is outraged that our government will not come to the aid of our citizens in their time of need. This is sad news but the news made us more determined to fulfill our mission. This is just another reason why we have to get rid of the present administration. This particular member informed us that some of the Joints Chiefs of Staff were overheard saying that if someone shot certain members of the administration, they will find some kind of medal to give to that person. This was good news for us. This information will aid us in our explanation to the Joint Chiefs of why we have organized a coup.

It is my turn. I am so nervous. I dimmed the lights again and on the screen a picture of the White House appears. It is a video with the flag blowing in the wind. As the flag flew I said, "I want to welcome you to my dream. I have for along time wanted to see America, where not only the people, but also our leaders brag about where they are from. We are suffering from a small amount of confusion in our policies. It seems that our leaders have chosen to help each other become the new millionaires of the country, and have overlooked the very people that put them in the positions they are in. They have taken advantage of us. They look us in the eye and lie to us. They violate our very freedoms that the Legislative Branch of the United States is supposed to protect. Washington D.C. has become the home for crooks protected by the establishment. As I think about the people that we will be removing from our Capitol, I cannot believe that a group of people can ignore the needs of most of the population of America. I think cold hearts is a requirement for citizenship here in this city. Greed has taken over the minds of good men. In a few days we are going to fire those good men and women and send them back home. Back home to the people that elected them, and the very same people that they screwed. But everyone knows very well what is happening. I do not have to tell any of you that. That is why we are here."

I walked over to the podium and grabbed my bottle of water. As I took a drink the screen changed from the White House to a map of Washington D.C. I waited a moment and said, "Gentleman this is our Capitol. This is the most corrupt and criminal city in America. Not only is a large portion of the population involved in criminal activities. But the main criminal element here is our politicians. You know the government employees that work within this city limits. In reality they are suppose to be the employees of the people of the various states that sent to Washington to represent their interest. Remember the phrase *taxation without representation?* I heard that phrase somewhere. Well, the truth is we are being taxed and taxed hard. But we still don't get any representation. So we are going to give these great men and women a vacation. Send them back to the place they call home. There, they can join the Taxpayers of America Association. If they live long enough, they will be eligible to pay taxes like everyone else. One of the first duties of the Internal Revenue Department will be to audit every government employee and private employee of any government official, to see if their bank account increased more than what they claim they earned. This distraction will help us in our journey. The public will want to hear about a politician that got thrown in jail for being a crook. The majority of Americans want some sort of justice. Many have suffered so long, and some of you here have too. Justice does not have to be perfect, but the people want something. As long as we do not make this a disaster, the people will accept it."

I walked over to the other side of the stage and turned toward the crowd and said, "This is why we have to make sure that everything that we do must stress safety for everyone. There are no enemies out there. We just experienced something that I cannot remember ever happening in our government. We all just witnessed a few people working on our economy and in a matter of a few minutes agree that we can fix our problem. We have all heard the saying "Take stock in America" and that is what is being proposed. Instead of our government taking over a company, we will do as the public does, by buying stock in the company. Then the government has a voice, but do not have total control. That is the way it should be."

As I look up to speak again there is a younger man with his hand up. That gave me a small startle and I simply said, "Yes". He asked, "I know this is off of the subject but what is this going to cost us? I mean how many lives is this going to cost us on both sides to try out our ideas? Everyone turned to look at him and I said, "That was my next subject. My purpose is to execute the mission with no one getting hurt or killed. This is my dream. And as you all know, dreams don't always come true. I have thought about this a lot. Whenever you have a crowd of people the chance for the *pack mentality* taking over is always possible. Then when you put millions of people, that are pumped up with the mission in mind, with weapons in their hands, someone has to get hurt either accidentally or out of rage. Everyone has to keep his or her composure. News of Park Police, Federal Agents, employees of our government, or any law enforcement officer being hurt or killed, is only going to cause us problems. And this violence will do us no good. People react to the way they are addressed. If you are firm but polite and do not intimidate a person, then negotiating with them is easier. Yelling and abusing people will only cause more rebellion amongst the population. We all got a first hand view of the union people trying to intimidate voters that attended some of our previous town hall meetings. That action, is what made me decide that we had to do something. Intimidating honest people that have the right to voice their opinion is the deciding factor for me. Make sure that you let everyone know that is in charge, to constantly talk with his or her people about maintaining a positive attitude. There is no hurry." I had never talked so much at one time in my life. And I had just gotten started.

As I reached again for my water bottle I said, "A few years ago I was a police officer in a small town. Not a whole lot went on there but we were getting a large population of immigrants moving into town because rent was cheap. As the older citizens passed on then the families usually rented out the homes. As the immigrants grew so did the crime rate. We had a Chief of Police and two officers. One was little ole' me. It was not uncommon to either get hit or pissed on every week. The job was not worth six bucks an hour." The crowd chuckled and then I continued, "I got jumpy when people seemed to be reaching for me, or something that an individual did that seemed threatening to me, would just trigger the self preservation mode. My Chief told me that it was not that I was abusive to people, but maybe I react too quickly. He constantly told me that it is better to talk for ten minutes than to fight for one. We need to practice that idea. Even though we will control the press initially, I would prefer that people did not hear that a number of people are hurt. These people with other agencies we are going to deal with have families also. Many of them are veterans and most are public servants. They do not deserve to get hurt and damn sure not killed. We will educate them to let them know our intentions at the beginning of our operation. The communications that we will have control of, as well as the airwaves, will happen before our intervention. As we are initiating our operation the officials will be watching and discussing our intentions. Each agency will get detailed advice on what to do. Most of the agencies role will be very simple. Our advice will be to do what they are paid to do and we will make America a good place to live again."

Before we closed the meeting for the evening a gentleman name Eric Leslie was asked to speak. Eric was a United States Attorney working at the Justice Department. He told us of government spying on their own legislative body by use of ONSTAR, and putting GPS units on their government and personal vehicles. If a case involving a government employee, or friend of the government came up, it all has to be cleared with the White House before an investigation can be launched, and before arrest and prosecution. Many members of the legislative branch of government are getting away with some serious crimes and violations, and are protected by the administration. Members of the Justice Department told him that some legislators have their homes and offices *bugged* in order for the administration to know any plans or feelings the opposition has. No one is safe from illegal wire tapping except for the criminals and terrorist. Nixon would have loved this time in our history. The White House has become extremely paranoid. The members of the administration want total control over all members of the government. Eric told us that many employees of the Justice Department want to quit, but are afraid to.

It is getting late and I have a ton of information to look over before we do any more briefings. We called the meeting until the next day, and this gives the people time to absorb what they have heard.

The next morning everyone is up early. Some have went for a morning swim in the cool water of the pool at the hotel. Many are in little groups having discussions. The morning will consist of getting organized on the shutdown of Washington D.C., and stopping all incoming and outgoing traffic in the city. James came over to the table I was at and said, "Come with us for a site-seeing trip. We want to take a close look at the places that we will block off to stop any and all access into the city." Myself and a couple of other people got up and followed him out to a SUV. It looks just like a federal vehicle. It is large, black, and has very tinted windows. You cannot see inside at all.

As we drive, we are talking about the details of our plan. One of the men working with the teams to shut down Washington is going over notes and looking at key places as we pass them, and occasionally is writing down notes. I am not looking at the scenery as much, as I am listening to everyone discuss plans on our mission. We pull over and James asked us to get out. I got out of the vehicle and James points across the street and says, "Welcome to the White House." As I look at this amazing building I am in shock. I have never been in Washington before and seeing the White House is very impressive. It is really more impressive in person than in any picture.

I look around and the town is busy. There is a lot of traffic, and tourists are leaning on the fence surrounding the property taking pictures. There are a couple of people with signs protesting something, but I am too busy to see what the signs say. We parked and took a walk down the Mall and got to the Washington monument. The Mall will be one of our staging areas. From there I can get an idea of the area that we are going to be at. We walk over to Independence Avenue, which is our planned parade route. We cross Seventh Street and stand in front of the Smithsonian National Air and Space Museum. No one in our little group has ever been inside the museum before, so we took a quick tour. This is definitely a building that when we control Washington I want to come back and spend more time. What this experience has done is show us how many visitors are in the city during the day. We will have to include plans to insure their safety and come up with a location where we can send them to be out of the way and make sure they will be safe.

The feeling of actually being at the location where we will make our stand is breath taking. Things are running through my mind, and for the first time I actually feel the full scope of this operation. How can we pull this off without the injury or death of someone? As my mind is wandering, James asked, "Anyone have any second thoughts?" He looks at each one of us and says, "Once it starts, we have to go through with it. If we balk at finishing our mission, I can assure you many of our people, as well as some citizens, will get hurt. Either we continue with a very good and organized plan, or we quit now. Which will it be?" As he looked at each one of us we all agreed to continue. The reality has hit me and hit me hard. There are times that it is hard for me to catch my breath. I am not afraid that something will happen to me but that innocent people will get hurt, and or we will fail in our mission.

After a brief look at Washington, I am determined that we have to preserve the city, so that future visitors can enjoy the sites and learn the history that is part of our country since the existence of the United States. To me having a city with all of this history and information available to the public, and yet be the most corrupt city with our officials is inexcusable. Our Capitol has the number one murder rate in the nation. It has the poorest schools. This shows me that our leaders do not care about anything except their own existence. How can they work in a city with the crime as bad as it is? How can they work and live in a city as filthy as Washington is? After my views of neglect of our Capitol, I am more determined to make our mission successful. Washington D.C. should be a place where anyone can come and not be in fear of being mugged, raped, or killed. It should be a city where children come to visit, and has a lasting memory on them so that they come back. It is the burial place of some of our bravest soldiers. It is a place where we should be able to stand in front of the Capitol or the White House and say, "This is where our dedicated leaders work and protect us and our freedom." Instead it is referred to a place where the criminals of the people conspire to screw the average American, and line their pockets with hard earned money that has been swindled from hard working Americans. The thought of a mass and public execution of all of our elected leaders has crossed my mind. Or should we send them to Guantanamo Bay for an extended vacation. Firing them seems to light of a sentence, but the outcome of our politician's criminal activities will have to be left up to our future leaders and government. It will be for them to deal with the situation.

We have an afternoon meeting that we all need to attend so we walk back to the vehicle and drive back to the hotel. The next time I see the White House will be under different circumstances. On the trip back we all are quiet except for few brief comments concerning different operations. We already have people in Washington watching and giving us information on different changes. It is finally coming together.

As we arrive back at our hotel, we go into the conference room and Josh, who is one of our military planners, inform us that all of the Guard and Reserve units will be secure by the time of our mission. Before the initiation of the coup, all governors will be notified that they have no more control over the assigned military units, and will be informed that the coup has already happened and that they shall continue on with their daily business. The notification will also tell them they will be contacted and informed so that we will have a smooth transition, as long as the individual states do not interfere, then the flow of funds from the federal government to their states will not be interrupted. Also measures are in place where all newspapers and media outlets will be temporarily controlled.

Once the meeting started we are informed about all activities concerning individual states. The states that are out of the continental United States, as well as Alaska, would not be affected due to their location. We do have followers in Alaska and Hawaii that will monitor those states. We will have control over one of the Guard Air Force units that is going to provide us with needed air cover from F-16's, and other aircraft, to primarily enforce the cancellation of air travel in the United States. The no fly policy worked well during the 911 attacks and shall work well during this mission.

The equipment that will be needed to block the access of Washington D.C. is in place and ready to be put into action. We will have an Abrams tank positioned at every road block as a show of force. We have just been informed that our military will be involved more than what we have thought. The reason the majority of our members were not told is so the mission will not be compromised. Once a member of our military is discovered as part of this, then treason can be charged. Not only do we not want to jeopardize the mission, we do not want to unnecessarily put our members in jeopardy. Military people will guard all of our facilities with orders from the Pentagon. It is nice to have good friends in high places.

We are told that we will have a surprise guest speaker. I have no idea who that is nor did James. When it come time for the guest speaker to come up we are informed that our plan had leaked out, and Israel has been informed of what we are doing. For the past couple of years the present Presidential administration has put Israel on the back burner, and the violence has escalated there and the Gaza Strip. This violence resulted in a staggering number of casualties for the people of Israel. The United States has almost abandoned one of its' most loyal allies. The existence of Israel is in jeopardy as long as the United States continues the policy it has with present day Israel. Our guest speaker is a member of the Israeli government. With him is a member of the Mossad.

The speaker states that the government of Israel will not physically participate in the coup, but will provide us with advice, and will help with the other countries. He told us that the Mossad has nearly one hundred agents on the ground in the Washington area as he spoke. They also can provide us with information on our government that they have learned from their private talks with our Secretary of State. Israel needs this change of government for their very existence. The speaker claims to be a relative of Lt. Col Yoni Netanyahu. He is the brother of Israeli Prime Minister Benjamin Netanyahu and is the only member of the Israeli Special Forces killed in the raid on Entebbe, Uganda. He remembers when the relationship between the United States and Israel was strong and each country did aid the other in covert activities. Under our present administration it has become hard for them to even get parts for the military equipment that we sold them. We assured them that the relationship will again be strong, and our military will be available to assist them when needed.

Israel has operatives all over the world and their intelligence agencies are the most successful in gathering good foreign intelligence. Since our Central Intelligence Agency has been turned into a Boy Scout camp instead of an information-gathering agency, we need valuable foreign intelligence. We will get first hand knowledge of reactions to our operation from the other countries. This information will come in very handy for our military leaders. With Israeli support our military will be more apt to listen to us. The Mossad has brought equipment that will jam radio waves. This will be very helpful to limit the communication between local and federal agencies in Washington.

Our last speaker of the day is a wealthy gentleman by the name of Gerald Watkins. Gerald is one of the businessmen that has been very successful in recruiting other wealthy people to help us with our endeavors. The wealthy business owners have been hurt by the new tax structures and many sold their businesses. Some just shut their businesses down. Occasionally when a union forced itself into a new company, many just shut the doors. With the new laws that have been initiated, this is about the only way to avoid being trapped into a union organization. Once the unions organized in a company, eventually they are running the company instead of the executive branch of that company. Listening to Gerald made me more determined to accomplish what we have started. A large number of wealthy people are in favor of having the administration, and a few legislative people assassinated if this does not work. No matter how it is to happen, certain public officials will not finish their terms, if we do not successfully fire them. America is tired of funding a few people with a desire to rob from everyone, and pocket the proceeds for themselves.

He told us about the large number of wealthy people that are in favor of our mission. Gerald stated that cash is stored in secure locations and ready for us if we need additional funding. The only thing that any of these donors want is to get rid of our present government and put in an honest group of people, and above all, educate the population on real facts and not lies. The lies from our politicians are part of the reason they are getting away with the corruption and abuse of their political powers. Many Americans just give up on trying to determine what is truth and what was lies from our politicians. Many Americans do not want to hear this crap from them anymore. This is a very easy thing to do. All one has to do is turn the television channel. As opposition slows to political policies, it makes the corruption easier to get away with. America is tired of that scenario.

It was time that we joined our people for the final planning stage.

CHAPTER 5

▼

IMPLEMENTING THE PLAN

It is time to start implementing our plan. The Civil War Re-enactment members are dealing with their own plans for their people. Initially, we went scouting and had plans to lease vacant land where tents could be put up and have lots of room for parking. We are planning on having more people than they have rooms in motels in the surrounding area.

It is not uncommon for the people that are part of the re-enactments, to drive two hours to get to a motel, and two hours back daily, when these activities are going on. Our initial planning is we will stage in a different area and bus many of the additional people in during the night for our mission. We already have box trucks reserved so they can bring any equipment that we need, as well as weapons. We made sure the plan did not put all weapons in one truck, and we have all equipment evenly distributed between trucks. Two trucks that are involved in the mission does not have anything in them in case a truck breaks down, we can simply unload the bad truck and load the good.

Most of the people will bring their own cars, and it will not be uncommon for rifles to be seen because we are conducting our activities right in with the prime hunting season of many surrounding states. Other than the increase of people, we want everything that we do to look as normal as it can be, while over populating an area. We have food tents, sleeping tents, portable toilets, and entertainment tents with satellite television. The one thing that is missing from our group is the children. Even the members of the re-enactment units left their children home. This is not going to be the place or time for children.

On a piece of property outside of Reston, Virginia, we have leased 220 acres of flat pastureland that is lined with a heavy row of trees. Unless a person is at the entrance to the property, you cannot even see anything other than trees. It is perfect. We will use this as a planning area and have several travel trailers parked there where we can meet and not be bothered. This is a beautiful area and in the evening in the cool winter air, you can appreciate the task that we are prepared to do. Most of us look at it as saving our country.

The people from the re-enactment units, that are part of our mission, will come and we will go over the details of our planned operation. One of the most detailed parts of the mission is the White House. The old man that supplied us with the plans of the tunnels under the White House and the Capitol are accurate from what we could tell. At the planned time of our event the President and Vice President are both going to be out of town. The family of the President is also going back to their private residence in Chicago and that is perfect. That will mean less security. That is ideal for me because I feel that if anyone will get hurt it will be at the White House.

One of our members is a former member of one of the independent contractor units that assisted our military when they go on overseas missions. In other words he is a mercenary. He made initial entry into one of the exits that are in the paperwork we got from the old man. This entry way or exit is inside of another structure that has a sheet of plywood nailed over it and just painted. The small structure that has the entryway door, appears that it has not been entered in years. The door on the building is rusted, and it has been a long time since this building has been opened up.

A large padlock is the only thing holding the metal door shut in the entryway. It is more of a bar door like a jail cell. Inside is an additional door that is solid metal and it has a regular door lock on it that is not locked. When our man opens the door he expects to see some type of security or hear some type of alarm. All he sees is years of dirt and spiders. No one has been in that area of the tunnels for years.

He come to report to us that he has actually entered the tunnels and got to the first place where the older doorways have been bricked over. He says the mortar has deteriorated so bad that he can actually remove bricks with a knife. He stopped short of opening up this doorway.

He watched the old building the next day to see if there was any activity at that location. No one even got close to the old building, which is overgrown mostly with brush and trees. Since no one showed up, he proceeded the next evening, and entered the bricked up wall. It is a vast tunnel and according to his GPS unit he has, he is very close to the underneath of the White House.

However he has traveled about four stories lower then he was when he first entered.

He comes upon another wall that has a grate up high near the ceiling and he can actually hear talking on occasions. According to the plans that were supplied to us, this tied into the new part of the tunnel that is still in use. It is believed that this part of the tunnel was filled in when a swimming pool was added to the White House. This is not the pool that was built in 1975 but the swimming pool that was built for President Roosevelt in 1933. It is now the pressroom. Since the original pool was built between the White House and the West Wing, he knows that he is close to where we need to be to actually gain entrance to the White House.

The plan calls for approximately two thousand men to storm the entrance gates during the parade along with entry under the White House. Gaining security for the White House is going to be a situation that will have a simple but dangerous plan. We want all of the security to concentrate on the activities outside and forget about the tunnels. We will take control of anyone that we see, and plan to gain access to the Secret Service office located somewhere inside.

It is imperative for us to communicate our intentions and let the officials know that we are not out to hurt anyone, but our mission is going to be accomplished. Our intentions are that there will be a pressroom with reporters there, so we can communicate with the country and inform them of our intentions, and we will request that the citizens understand that this is to be a peaceful coup and not a violent one.

Then one our members brought up the history of some takeovers, and as we studied how the coups were accomplished, we learned we did not even need to take over the White House. All we need to do is let people come out of the building, but let no one in. After all this is the house of the people and not the President's personal property. This will surely help eliminate the possibility of someone getting injured or killed. What I did not know is that plans have already been put in place for the White House.

This change of plans is one of many that we will have to decide on very fast. I hate to do things at the last minute, but safety is imperative. The public perception will be better for us if the citizens do not see armed men storming the White House.

The information we received about the tunnels will be very useful so that entry cannot be gained through those places and therefore the people inside will be limited to the time they can stay in there, because they will not receive food or needed things. We can manage the country and start the re-building process by using the Capitol building.

At this time we have many people in the area that are believers in what we plan to do. Some do not really believe it but just like a pack of wolves, many will follow when the event starts. We mainly have to control that factor and not let it turn into a pack mentality. Destruction and violence is not going to be allowed. After all, this is all about our country and we are there to fix our government. We are not doing this to destroy anything.

We arrived at our staging area. It is great to see that everyone is in a good mood and laughter can be heard abound. There are small groups of people going over their individual duties, and some people are just killing time, so to speak. As we walk around to inspect the different facilities and I personally am impressed at what I see. It reminds me of the military with everything lined up perfectly and organized. There are electric lines running over the ground feeding electricity to various tents and facilities. There is a refrigerator truck loaded with meat and we actually have butchers cutting meat on a band saw. Large grills for smoking meats are lit and all kinds of beef and pork are being smoked. The air is filled with the smell of food.

In order for it to look authentic there are hundreds of tents for the re-enactment soldiers. In front of the tents are rifles stacked in a circle. We have various cannons and even our little 105 mm Howitzer is there under a tarp. Men are running around in both Union and Confederate uniforms from the Civil War time.

I noticed a unique thing. On the property is a large water storage tank, which is in working order. A platform has been assembled on the ground close to the tank that holds a large number of swimming pool solar panels. They are circulating the water in the tank absorbing heat and transferring it to the water stored in the tank. It provides for warm water for showers and cleaning but the water is not real hot. The temperature is just warm enough to knock off the chill of a cold shower. It is not warm enough for someone to stay in very long like we do at home, but it is nice in our situation.

When we started, we received some military radios we can use for our communications that are on a totally different frequency than what military, air traffic, and law enforcement uses, and will not be affected by the jamming equipment. There is a communication tent that consists of communication and Internet service also. Most of our communication with other units is going to be through the Internet. We have acquired a couple of news satellite trucks that are capable of satellite communications, and will also serve us as our broadcasting platform. The Israelis have provided us with a little device that can jam the satellite waves also if we need it.

A twenty-foot by forty-foot tent is at one location that is constructed over a large hole to bury trash. We have to hide it so officials can not see an illegal dumping site. It will be unfortunate to have some code enforcement officer stumble on to our trash pile and mess up our plans. In front of this tent is a person guarding it and a sign was posted that stated, "Women's Dressing Tent." We did on occasions have local electric service people come by to check on our temporary electrical hookup, as well as other county personnel. Everyone has been instructed to be polite and helpful to these people. We do not want to draw unwanted attention to anything. I learned that a good way to make someone feel comfortable, and not suspicious, is to offer them a beer, and asked them to sit a while.

I was told there are a couple of state troopers that will drive through from time to time. We have police officers in our group and one of them had a great idea. Upon leaving this place was a DUI checkpoint using our police officers. The purpose of this is two fold. The main reason is to keep anyone that has been drinking on the property and not drive on the roads. This not only prevents endangerment to the population, but also prevents a person under the influence of alcohol from leaving and possibly talking to the wrong person, or saying the wrong thing. On the other hand it makes an appearance to state and local law enforcement that we are responsible. This simple procedure reduces our visits from the police. The downside is sometimes an officer will stop by just to bullshit with our police officers. The visits do keep everyone on their toes.

In the evening, our people will project a movie onto the side of a white box truck. People gather and enjoy some relaxation. It is amazing how a simple projector and a laptop computer can turn the night into a location for entertainment. We have stationed other people with night vision devices on top of the other trucks to keep constant surveillance on the surrounding area. One of the main reasons is to make sure that none of our people are sneaking out to meet with law enforcement, or that some spy will not enter the location to attempt to gather information. We have gone too far to have our mission fail at this time. The closer that we get to our hour of independence, the more security we need. We have armed contractors in the tree line in case we have a problem. Luckily other than a few curious deer that are evading the yearly hunt, the nights are peaceful. They are also pretty chilly.

I am enjoying walking around and talking with people from different parts of the country. After the end of the movies, many people are winding down and hitting the sack. I am ready to crawl into my RV, take a shower, have a drink or two or three, and get some sleep. Then we hear a truck coming in the entrance, and I was curious on who it can be at this late hour. As I started walking toward the truck, the individuals that are stationed at the entrance escorted the truck to an area that is about in the middle of the property. As the truck came my way I noticed an Abrams tank riding on the back of this large military transport. My adrenalin started to flow. One of the men came over and said that it was going to be used in the parade. He says the tank personnel are part of our mission and the tank will be trucked to its' location when needed. It is an awesome site. A uniformed man named Lt. Johnson is in charge of the tank and he come over to talked with us. The parade is set up so the Civil War group will be in front and then some newer military equipment will follow. Our little 105 mm Howitzer will be part of that parade.

After a brief chat, I decide that I can look at the tank in the morning when we can see it well, and I am going to get some sleep. I get into my RV, take off my shirt, and fix myself a drink. After a few minutes I can hear horns honking and people yelling. I get up and go outside. One of our security people come over to me and tells me that there has been a car crash only a quarter of a mile away. The car has gone down a hill and it is reported that there is severe injuries. That is all we need.

I got our people to get our medical team up to see if they can help. I go with a couple of men to see what we can do. When we get there, the car is lodged between two trees. A woman is injured but we can not get to her. We have no equipment to extricate her. What we need is to get the car up on higher ground. We need one thing that we do not have and that is a tow truck. I sent a man back to the camp to see if he can maybe find us a large four-wheel drive pickup with a chain or cable. As I am trying to find a truck that can pull the car up word got out to the tank crew. Their tank is equipped with a winch for towing heavy equipment. The tank personnel fired up the Abrams and swung it around on the trailer and just took off. This thirty-ton piece of metal jumped off the trailer instead of being removed the normal way. We can hear this monster coming full speed down the highway. About the time the first state trooper got here the tank is swinging around and backing down the hill. The crew grabs the cable and takes it to the car. One of the men hooks a chain onto the underside of the car and attaches it to the cable wench. With a simple hand signal the Abrams turbine engine comes alive and the wench starts pulling. The hill is steep, but it is a pretty level surface so the car is not bouncing, but steadily comes toward the highway.

When the car got to more of a level ground the wench stops and everyone runs to see if they can get the woman out of the car. Our medical team was checking her vitals and tells us she needs help fast. We still cannot get the doors open. The tank crew brings down a chain and wrapped it around the door of the car. They take another chain and hooks to the frame on the other side and then attaches it to a nearby tree. Once again the turbine engine comes alive but this time the gun turret is turning toward the car. As the barrel of the tanks' gun is facing the car the crewmember wraps the chain around the barrel of this big gun. Again with a simple hand signal the turret starts turning the opposite way. As the chain tightens it rips the door right off of the hinge. Now the driver is exposed so the medical team can remove her.

We have a collapsible military stretcher. They put the lady on the stretcher and say they have to get her to the medical tent. She is placed on the back of the tank and slowly they climb the hill and proceed down the road. This time we have a police escort. As they approach the medical tent, I can see that it is in full operation. People are scrabbling and it looks like a scene from an emergency room television show. The tank comes to a stop, men grab the stretcher, and take it to one of the tables they have set up. Immediately there are medical personnel cutting off clothing and inserting IV's into this injured lady. While they are working on the patient, we all watch as they vigorously worked to keep her alive. Even though many of these people have never worked together, and especially in an emergency situation, the procedures went on like a military planned exercise.

About this time we can hear a siren from the distance. The ambulance is on the way. It is directed to the medical tent and we to clear the way for it to be able to back up to the tent. Once again the Abrams fired up and this time slowly moved back to the truck it had come in on. This time the trailer has to be dropped before the tank can be loaded. It cannot crawl upon the trailer the way it came off. While the ambulance personnel are assisting the medical team, I go over to the tank to thank them. That is when we almost have a serious problem.

The state trooper drives over to the tank to get some information, crawls up on the tank, and looks in the hatch. That is when he sees the live ammunition. He jumped back and starts asking all kinds of questions, and is very nervous. Lt. Johnson is a very cool guy. He calmed the trooper down and says, "You have just seen something that the Homeland Security Department does not want you to know about. As the trooper started to speak, Lt. Johnson says, "Since 911 there are, many pieces of military equipment that are loaded in case of an emergency. The first thing is that you are not suppose to know about it, and I am not suppose to let you see it." The trooper said, "What would stop you from using that damn tank to hold up the corner store?" "Our guns are computer operated. When the gunner locates a target he has to put in an access code or the gun will not fire. It will do everything it is supposed to except fire. We do not have that code. The Pentagon gives it to us when we need it. Tonight my career is over because of our little rescue mission. When my commander hears about me using this tank to pull that car, and then you seeing these rounds, I am history if not put in chains." The trooper calmed down and it seemed as if he was in deep thought. He looked at Lt. Johnson and says, "I will leave the information about the tank out of my report. If it comes up I will just say I did not think it was relevant to the accident." Johnson replies, "Thanks. I appreciate that." As he walks off the trooper turned and says, "My Major most likely will not believe it anyway. Who would he call to verify that?" Lt. Johnson yells, "The White House." With that both men go their own way.

About this time the ambulance is leaving the scene. Our medical staff has saved the woman's life. Doing a good thing and saving a life is a good sign for our mission. I just want to get to my RV and have a drink to celebrate. I am in need of a shower. I am in need of some sleep. This shows us that at any time, there can be an unforeseen problem that may have to be dealt with. This time it is our military counter parts that save us. I hope that our luck will continue with professional responses to upcoming problems.

The next morning I wake up at the sound of a trumpet. I forgot that I am in a camp with military people. It is okay. I have actually got about two and a half hours of sleep. A good cup of coffee will wake me up. All I have to do is find my pants so I can walk to one of the food tents. It appears that the many drinks I had to get me to fall asleep, have not cleared my system at this time. I never get hangovers, but I do suffer from lack of energy at times. This cannot be one of those times. Too much is at stake to not be clear headed.

I locate the closest food service tent and proceed directly to the coffee pot. Oh, it is a glorious sight. I grab a cup of coffee and head out the door to an outside table so I can also have a smoke. I have a routine that I have no control over. It is coffee, cigarette, and bathroom. Sometimes it is not in that order. But it is guaranteed to happen. After my routine, then I can adapt to almost anything.

I walk back to the RV and got ready for the day. I have to shave and brush my teeth. On the way out of the food tent I refilled my coffee cup. The coffee is strong and effective. It has woke me up and has gotten my bodily functions to perform as usual. Now I can pretend to be ready for the day.

When I walk out of the door of my RV I look across the vast property and see Union Soldiers and Confederate Soldiers all standing at attention as they raised Old Glory. In the center of the property is this very large Abrams tank. The tank crew stands on top of the tank saluting the flag. The barrel of the gun is elevated at its' highest trajectory. What is amazing is that one piece of equipment is about equal to all those people and our other equipment. The most feared military tank in the world is sitting in front of me waiting to take on the very government that approved its' existence. What a sight and I will be damned. I did not even bring a camera.

As I watch the morning proceedings, James walks over and asks, "Did you get enough sleep?" I looked at him and say, "You have got to be kidding." As he stuck his hand out for a morning shake he says, "Our new government has just save the first life. You know, depending on how a person values life, if we stopped right know and went home, we will be ahead of the game. We can actually say that we won. But we both know that we are just starting. It is a great way to start." James waives and walks off.

I finish my morning ritual and proceed to the tank. Lt. Johnson is standing beside it on the trailer supervising the daily maintenance. I yell out, "Lieutenant." He looks over to me and says, "Good morning, Sir." I walk up to the trailer and ask, "How does it feel?" and he stops me there. He says, "I am sorry for jeopardizing the mission. A few people have jumped on me this morning." I ask him, "Well you saved a life. Which is more important?" He asks, "Your are not upset? Did I make the right decision?" I said, " You tell me. Your decision, according to the doctors, is that your quick response did save that woman's life. You made a decision that kept this woman from bleeding to death. You tell me if you made the right decision?"

He stood there for a minute thinking about his answer. Before he could say anything I say, "If we have problems with the law enforcement, we will just start early and take them in custody. We are not trying to take over a country by force resulting in casualties on either side. I want to have no casualties. You proved that you can make a decision from your heart and not your macho. I have a belief that you are going to go far in the military." He snapped back with a question, "But what about the mission comes first?" I had to think about that for a minute and then I gave him two answers." First of all the mission has not officially started. Second the mission at the time was to free that woman from that car. In reality our mission is to save the citizens of this country, and attempt to protect them until a sound government of loyal people takes over. You saved your person. Now I have to save mine." With that I wave over my shoulder as I walk off. It is time for another cup of coffee.

As I enter the food tent, I notice Jim is standing there. I have not seen him for some time because we are working on different projects. I yell, "Jim." He looks up and says, "Here is the son-of-a-bitch that got me into this mess." He walks over to me with his hand out and says, "Well we are in this up to our ass this time. At least the food is good." I ask him how he is and he tells me that he is ready to get this over with and return to normal. I do not know for sure what normal is. I look at him and say, "Well it will be over soon. At least the initial stage will be over. It will be the most challenging. After that I have to rely on people that have the ability to persuade people instead of using force. In a few days my usefulness will be over too." He looks at me and ask, "Won't you be on the staff when this all takes affect?" I reply, "Hell no! I am no politician. Running a country is far out of my league. I will see you when we get home." With that I left.

I continue to my RV and once I enter I think, "What am I going to do when this is over?" I do not have an idea. I guess go back to work and try to act as if nothing happened. What a strange feeling I have. For the first time I think I should have a backup plan in case our mission fails, and the whole world comes after us. I just might have to move to Israel.

Today is going to consist of the final planning stage. We will analyze the information that we are receiving from our people located all over Washington. So far, the information is in line with what we have planned, except for the large amount of tourist that is in town. I guess they are going to stay for the parade. That is okay, but more tourists mean more children. Extra care is going to have to be implemented to insure their safety. The extra people will aid us in the actual count of people involved.

An idea has come up between our military officers and the other staff involved in the planning. This idea has come from a time when Roosevelt was President. A declaration of martial law can be forwarded to all the Governors of each state. The reason will not have to be given except that our country is under a grave threat. The declaration will provide limited information to the Governors. They decide to include the fact that all Guard and Reserve units will be under the control of the Pentagon and trespassing on these properties could result in lethal action. This way we will not have any problem with state and local law enforcement. The details of the threat will not be included for security reasons. Because of this threat the airwaves will be shut down. Only government controlled press, radio and television will be operating. This will explain the reason that air traffic is cancelled as well as the lack of communication from Washington to each state. Under this declaration we will have some panic. When the people have no idea what type of threat we are under, then it will be hard for the individual citizen to know what to panic over. This come somewhat late in the game, but seems to be a great plan, if we can get it into action. The Homeland Security Department will have to give some partial reason to each state to keep the officials of the state from realizing what is happening.

There are big advantages to this idea. As long as each individual state is made aware we are under federal martial law, then law enforcement will be occupied making sure curfews are being enforced. Criminal activities will be reduced greatly because no one would be allowed out on the street. The television channels will only show a banner that states that we are under martial law. Only the stations that we are using to release information, will be allowed on the air. For people who are familiar with United States law concerning martial law, it goes back to the passage of the Posse Comitatus Act in 1878. This act forbids military involvement in domestic law enforcement unless Congress approves it. The people that have powers to oppose us will assume that either there is a possible invasion, a direct threat for the safety of the public, or rebellion. They will assume that Congress voted, and approved this measure. The authority we have will use martial law and will fall into this doctrine. We are concerned about public safety, our safety, and there damn sure is a rebellion. Since we are firing Congress, there is no need for them to vote on the issue. Our take over of the Congress will give consent to the military to perform their action. That is if they go along with the idea.

This idea has come late, but it will solve many problems for us. The unknown is what we are afraid of. Our main problem will be timing. At the time we pick for our mission to start, we have to notify the states, contact the FAA to cancel all flights, stop the television and radio stations from broadcasting, and take control of Washington. With our government television broadcast we can show the shutdown of Washington D.C. and the Abrams tanks blocking the roads. Who will suspect anything wrong, other than what we are telling the public. We will never name the threat, but provide information to the public for their safety. Stay home will be the theme that we will advise the public, and let them know if they get caught out during this time of martial law, they will go to jail, and possibly get shot. This will be the least fearsome thing that we can do for the public. We want them out of our way to avoid unwanted involvement from the individual states and the public. This will be a perfect time for the American public to have another child. If you have to stay home you might as well enjoy the time. Thousands of people could say a few years from now that they were conceived during the coup.

While the planning committee is busy at work trying to make sure that they can pull this off, I have some spare time on my hands. I always have a hard time being idle. It is too early to take a nap, so I take off for a walk of the property. I am coming up on one of the food tents when I look over and noticed the men with the Abrams. I grab an armful of water bottles and head their way. They are bored to death. I am becoming that way fast so I can understand. That is the one thing that I hate about the military. It is always hurry up and wait. A soldier can get pumped up and burn him or her out by waiting. Then when that burned out feeling happens your mind wonders. I do not want the tankers to have wondering minds. As I approached the truck carrying the tank I witness the tank driver and gunner having a conversation. When they see me they act very nervous. I can only imagine that they are having second thoughts. They are tired and have time to think about what they are doing. This can possibly be a bad conversation.

I walk up to them and yell, "Catch." Both of the men turn around as I toss them a bottle of water. Before they can say anything I blurt, "I will be glad when this is over so we can go home." The tank driver faced away from me and says, "Yeah we probably will never see home. Prison walls will be about what we face." This confirms to me that they are thinking way too much. I chuckled and say, "You will see home but the rest of us may not." He turns and looks at me and says, "What makes you think we will see home?" I thought about that for just a second and reply, "You are under orders, and we are under our own ambition."

While he was considering an answer I yell, "Lt. Johnson. Can you come over here for a minute please?" As the Lieutenant walks over to me I say, "I think we are having second thoughts." The Lieutenant looks at them but before he could say anything I ask, "Do you have orders to be here?" He says, "Sure I do but you know how we got them." I ask, "Are they written orders?" He says, "Yes they are and we all have a copy." I look over to the two men and ask, "What are you afraid of? You have orders to be here. And we all know that you do not question orders from your superior. Am I right?"

With that question they have a serious look on their face and the gunner says, "Those orders are no good." I snapped back, "How the hell do you know that? How would you be able to know that? I may be a plant to make sure you follow your orders, and may be reporting back to your superior. You have a better chance by following the orders, than you do refusing to obey an order." Lt. Johnson says, "No one will know that you are aware that the orders or false. That is unless you say something. That is why everyone has a copy. If you get taken into custody they will find the orders, and assume you were just obeying orders that you got from me. And my orders came from the top individuals that will have problems long before we will if things go wrong." I gave Lt. Johnson a bottle of water and as I walk away I say, "You guys locked in your fate last night. Who will think that you are doing what we are going to do, when you jeopardize everything by saving that woman's life? A person that is about to attempt what we plan would be crazy to do what you did for fear of getting caught. All you have to tell anyone is that you are obeying written orders. Besides, fairly quickly we will do our thing and it will be successful and you guys will get a medal for what you did. We got you here didn't we? If we did not have good planning could we put together all of this?" As I walk away I am pointing across the property. From their view all they see was a massive amount of people. It is truly amazing that we are able to get all of these people here. And this is only one of many campsites, and don't forget about the thousands and maybe millions of people that are on their way. This is a truly amazing sight all right.

The next morning will be the first day of the re-enactments. They are scheduled to be in many locations around Washington. An extra meeting is planned later on in the evening, and I have been asked to be there. I think I will take a shower and have a cup of coffee and relax before we start. I have developed a large case of butterflies ever since I realized that the tank operators have their doubts about what is about to happen. If men that are trained for dangerous situations are having problems coping with reality, then what about the thousands of people that are assembled on this property site? Maybe they have not realized the full danger of what we are about to do. We just need another twenty-four hours, and then it will not matter who knows. Once this starts it will be over fast. I know that more of our military is going to be involved because the plans have changed. There will be no guards or personnel stationed at the Pentagon. The top minds in our establishment do not feel that the Pentagon needs to be watched, and or overtaken so that must mean that we have them as allies. That will be a blessing in disguise.

As time gets closer to our meeting, I head to the food tent. It is a night of celebration. It is the eve of a coup against the most powerful country on the face of the earth. The whole world will be watching to see what will happen to America. The attitude of the people is outstanding. No one seems very nervous. Mainly because they have been so busy. The cooks have fixed a feast. There is steak, pork, chicken, different vegetables, yeast rolls, mashed potatoes, and three different kinds of gravy. As I look down the food line I see a large salad bar. At the end if the salad bar is various pies and cakes. That is the smell that covered the property earlier in the day. The only problem I have is that I do not have much of an appetite.

Even though it seems like we should be happy and ready for action, it really is sad that we have to do this. But we do feel that it is the only way to save America from being destroyed by political criminals. The average American is suffering because of a few crooks. I stand here looking at a great amount of food and I wonder how many people across our great country will not have a good meal this evening. How many children will go to bed tonight hungry? How many will wake up in the morning, and not have anything for breakfast? This is not supposed to happen in America. I grab a cup of iced tea and head toward our meeting place. While I am walking I see multiple vehicles heading toward our tent that we meet in. I am curious who was in those vehicles.

I walked into the tent and there are many high-ranking military officers from all branches of service at the front of the tent. James is with them and he looks up, sees me, and motioned for me to join him. Here I go heading to the front of the tent wondering if something is wrong? Instead everyone seems to be serious but cordial. James starts introducing me to everyone as the author of this mission. I do not want to be seen as the instigator of a coup. In reality, if I had not gone to Jim and opened my mouth, I may not be in this position. I may have prodded the idea some, but I am surely not the only one with the desire for change. And this time, it will be good change for everyone.

It is time to take a seat and get the meeting started. As I am looking around the room, I notice that this meeting has armed military guards at the exits and throughout the tent. This is the first time weapons have been in one of our meetings. Before my mind starts to wonder, James opens up the meeting. "May I have you attention?" James says. The room turned quiet. As James introduces the various military, federal, and other people that will have something to say this evening a warm feeling came about the interior of the tent.

A two star Air Force General walked to the podium. He says, "It is a good thing that I judge this army by the heart and not the appearance. Some of the clothes people wear out here are a hundred years old." With that comment he got a pretty good laugh. Many people in the tent were in Civil War wardrobe. Two soldiers brought in a tripod with some charts on it. The General says, "Let me show you what we have so far. At 1400 hours tomorrow the United States will come to a halt, as we know it. A communication will go out to all state capitols and every law enforcement agency in the United States informing them that the White House has ordered martial law. The only thing that they will be told initially is that there is a grave threat to the security of the United States. We will not tell them that we are the threat. The Pentagon will notify all the Governors that the Guard and Reserve units will be under the command of the United States military. The members of these units will be notified that they are on alert but will be ordered to stay away from the facilities until notified. Every law enforcement agency in the United States that has a phone or fax will be notified to enforce martial law in their jurisdiction. At the same time all radio and television transmissions will stop. Satellites will be jammed to help with this mission, but we only have a few hours that we can do that. The Vice-President will be in Iraq with our soldiers. The President will be at Camp David with his family. There he will stay until we transport him back to his personal residence. The Joints Chiefs of Staff have already taken control of the nuclear weapons. We are in full control of the nuclear arsenal. The Guard units from Texas, California, Arizona and New Mexico will be deployed to the Mexican border along with the A-10 attack aircraft from Davis-Monthan Air Force Base in Arizona. A unit of Cobra Helicopters will join them in the mission of closing our borders. Those units have already been put on alert status awaiting orders. This will not be a good time for the drug smugglers to attempt to cross the border. Support aircraft will be in place and if a rabbit tries to run toward the border of the United States we will see it. People crossing the border during this time, and until we deem necessary, will be subject to a zero tolerance policy of trying to enter the United States. Illegal entry will not be tolerated. The Reserve units will take over the ports of entry along the coast.

As of tomorrow evening there will not be one shipping container that will not be opened and searched until it is deemed necessary to discontinue the inspections. Other Guard units will assist the Reserve units. We will keep these units very busy. If they are concentrating on their mission, they will not be involved in ours. No one will be told of the basis of the threat. All other military units presently located in the United States will be put on alert and monitored by the Pentagon. It is our wish that the actual coup will be performed by your organization instead of the military. After this is over we do not want the appearance that our military was involved other than with the current war efforts and the security of the United States."

The General turned to an Admiral of our Navy and he nodded and approached the podium. He takes out some notes and says," By 1400 hundred hours tomorrow there will be a blockade of maritime shipments to the United States. No ship will be allowed to come closer than one hundred miles from the shores of the Continental United States. No foreign military ship will be allowed to come closer than two hundred fifty miles from the shores of America. Every ship from the United States Navy, as well as the United States Coast Guard, will protect our coast, except for a few that are needed for direct support of our troops participating in the current military actions. At this same time every foreign nation will know that this is not the time to screw with us. Any vessel that approaches an American ship will be eliminated. All foreign nations will be advised that the arsenal of nuclear weapons of the United States will be under the control of the United States military. When they hear that the civilians are out of the loop as far as nuclear deployment is concerned, we should have no problem with any nation other than a lot of verbal crap from our enemies. Our allies will be briefed, and assured, our intentions will be concentrated on our country. I really do not see any problem from anyone. Most foreign countries will have a loss for words when they get the word that a coup has happened in the United States. Some may see it as a ploy, but our information tells us that there is not a nation that will try to take advantage of our situation, as long as it does not go on for very long. Other than satellite phones, all cell phone use will stop at 1300 hours. The FAA will force all planes to land at 1400 hours, and this should not take longer than an hour and a half. The overseas flights that take off earlier will be allowed to land unless we have concerns. Navy fighters will escort those planes to their landing destination. No private or commercial aircraft will be allowed to take off after 1400 hours. The world as we know it will come to a halt at 1600 hours when the national curfew takes place. These times are Eastern Standard times." I am having a hard time writing all of this down. For security reasons there are no printed versions of their briefings.

As the Admiral walks away from the podium, a Colonel from the Army walks up and says, "I guess that by our presence you can tell that the military will have a larger role in this mission than you may have originally thought. I want to go over with you some more details. For those of you that are located in the other areas, a briefing will be held at each one of them in the morning with final plans. Here is where we are at the present time. From this time forward no one will be able to leave the staging areas. We are on lock-down. If a medical emergency arises, and our facilities here cannot take care of it, a military chopper will evacuate the injured or ill to a military hospital. It is imperative that you let all of your people know that the armed guards at each compound have the authority to use deadly force. They are here for your support, and will not, tolerate any harassment. So far we have had only one injury regarding weapons. A man had his hand damaged while trying to clean a loaded musket, but he will be okay. It is a miracle that we have not had any more than that. The city of Washington D.C. will be locked down by your members, but will be assisted by the military. The military will be in control over details, and must be obeyed. This is not to undermine you, but to make sure that no innocent person will be hurt. A military uniform has more status than an old Confederate or Union uniform. With our presence the chance of having a problem with local, state, or federal agencies will be eliminated. We will have full measures of security at the Pentagon, and request that your people are not there. We are on the same side, but in order for this to work out, we will need no interference at the Pentagon and its' personnel. We will be extremely busy with the foreign affairs issues, and monitoring our ongoing campaigns in the combat zones. We are working on some legal issues and the military may activate all of the Guard and Reserve units to help us. The Joint Chiefs will determine this. Absolutely, there will be no cameras and no pictures or videos taken of the on goings. This is for all of our protection, and also, if someone is seen taking pictures then they will be taken into custody and turned over to the military. We do not want to have photographers assaulted, but we do need to find out what pictures they have taken and why."

He walks over to the other two military officers and talks with them for a few minutes. He comes back to the podium and pulls out a piece of paper and says, "That will be it until the morning briefings. These people I need to stay behind for an additional meeting." He starts calling names and mine is called. As the room clears I just sat there thinking about what was going to take place the next day. What have I got myself into with all of these other people? Thoughts are running through my head so fast I cannot separate them. I wonder what the morning will bring.

As he approaches the podium again he says, "Things as you know it, has escalated in the last seventy-two hours. It appears that our President has stepped over his boundary and if he continues our whole military will be at risk. All of these Executive orders have endangered our security, and will limit our ability to monitor terrorists, and other undesirable groups. In an agreement with the Taliban, he is planning on releasing all of the prisoners from Gitmo here. We will soon have three hundred of the most dangerous people, that have one thing on their mind walking our streets. Destroy America. There have been numerous terrorist attempts to enter the U.S. by air, and it is unknown how many may attempt to cross the border from Mexico. But as we speak, eight A-10's are being armed. They will be in the air before our mission starts and if all goes well they will be backed up by F-16's and F-18's from Florida. We will finally shut the border between Mexico and the United States down. The Mexican military will receive a letter by 1400 tomorrow that will let them know that if any of their police or military try to cross the border, to deliver drugs or people, they will be fired up on, and we will consider this an act of war." Joe asks, "We have been fighting a war for years on the border of Iran, and we cannot keep explosives and people from crossing into Iraq. What makes you think that we can secure the Mexican border?" The Colonel replies, "That is because we are not allowed to stop the flow of terrorist and equipment. We made a poor attempt at it, but our orders are not to get Iran too upset, even after we destroyed half of their country. I can assure you that nothing will come close to that border that we will not see. We have been able to spot border crossers for years, but the Border Patrol was limited from high up in the administration. I guess even an illegal alien is a potential voter for someone." Everyone chuckled at that, but it is fact.

The Colonel turned the meeting over to another man that only identified himself as Gerald. Gerald approached the podium and says, "Well, we have someone in every federal agency, but we have one agency that will be a problem. That is the Secret Service. They will stick to the President like glue. We will limit their ability to put choppers in the air as well as aircraft. This is where our officials at the Pentagon will come in handy. They can guard the President all they want to, but he will no longer be the President. He will be able to receive Secret Service protection because he was a President, and if they want to, they can take him to where ever. But he will not be allowed to stay at Camp David. That brings up another problem. We were not told that the Prime Minister of Russia was at Camp David, until we got word from one of the Marine pilots. It will be imperative that we handle this situation, instead of any of your people. This will require a very diplomatic approach. Maybe a quart of Vodka will do the trick. No matter what, the Prime Minister will be allowed to leave and return to his country. He will have a fighter escort all the way to the Russian border. His safety is one thing, but our need to show that we are still in operation will be necessary. Okay that will do it for this evening. We will have a breakfast meeting at 0730 hours in the morning, and prepare for a very busy day. I hope everyone gets a good night sleep. Good evening." With that comment he walks off and we disburse.

CHAPTER 6

▼

TIME TO REFLECT

When I leave the tent, I again look across the vast acres of our camp. I take in all of the sights. There is now more of a military presence here than before, and I can see the sentries being taken to their assigned locations. Thousands of people are enjoying a cool evening, and there are many campfires. With the breeze we have, the smoke from the fires does not settle on the property, but the smell of a good campfire is a welcome thing. It always is fun to sit in front of a campfire when there is a chill in the air. The sound of conversation and laughter, could be heard all over the camp. Even some music from portable radios can be heard.

I wander over to the food tent and grab a bite to eat. The cooks have assembled a feast of barbeque, vegetables, dinner rolls, and deserts. Just about anything that you can imagine to go along with a meal of this caliber, was on the serving tables. The state troopers have dropped by to have a free meal. The appearance by law enforcement does not faze anyone and many people are having conversations with them. The troopers got up and thanked everyone, and one of the officers said he had to go find a tree to hide behind, so he could sleep off the meal. The troopers have no clue about what is going on. All they are aware of is that we have our people contained, and the military have positioned some troops to guard the tank and other equipment, that is scheduled to be in the parade.

While enjoying the cool air, I grab a cup of coffee, and head toward the tank. As I walk out of the tent, I reach into a cooler, to grab a six-pack of beer. I approach the tank and say to the driver, "Here you might as well have a cold one before they execute us for treason." They laugh and I ask Lt. Johnson if they can have a beer, and he nods to them. I start asking them questions about the Abrams tank, and I soon find out how proud these guys are to be part of a tank unit. The gunner motions for me to come to the rear of the tank and points and says, "We thought we would change the name." On the rear of the tank painted in white letters is "Glory Bound". I think this is an appropriate name. What it shows me is that the men are focused and are ready for the mission. I asked Lt. Johnson, if what he told the State Trooper the night before about the code to fire, was correct. He tells me that he made it up, but it was all he could think of at the time. I chuckled and say, "Good job Lt. Johnson, Good job."

I bid them good night and start walking back toward my RV. I am lucky that the motor home that I am using has a satellite antenna, and I can receive television channels. I tune it in to a local news channel. Reporters are talking about two murders today, and multiple robberies around our nations capital. I spend the next few minutes flipping channels listening to news from around the country. It is all sad news, and there is not one good news story. About that time I heard a knock at my door.

I get up to open the door. Here stands a man I have talked with numerous times before. He asks if he can come in and talk. His name is Hank. I say, "What brings you to my world Hank?" He replies, "Are you nervous about tomorrow?" As I closed the door behind him I motioned for him to have seat. I look at the television and say, "Look at all this crap that occurs on a daily basis. We are lucky that we live in a smaller town instead of one of the big cities. And to answer your question, yes I am scared of the unknown. We seem to have most of everything under control, and with the military taking on more of a role, it helps me relax some."

Hank says, "I never imagined that we would actually get this far. I look out there and see all of these people, and I have a hard time believing that there are even more people participating in this thing that are not here. Are the other camps this full of people?" I look up and say to him, "I hear that they are just as full, and many more people are on their way." We sat and watched a few minutes of news, and there was not one good story, except for another Governor getting busted for bribery. That makes my night. We watch a news report of our President having a news conference from Camp David. He is still blaming all our problems on the previous administration, as he has done from day one of his presidency. Even supporters of his are tired of hearing all of this blame crap. Americans have heard excuses, promises, and the usual numerous lies, and hardly ever get to see any results. Hank says, "I guess we can only improve things. Right now they are all screwed up here." Hank get ups, shakes my hand, and thanks me, and leaves.

As I reflect on the actions that I have taken to get this far into this operation, I use the news reports I am watching to confirm what we have set out to do as just and needed. A story came on about the war in Afghanistan and they are reporting a major offensive has just taken place. The embedded reporter that is assigned with our soldiers said earlier in the day they were ordered to this location, and once there, all hell broke loose. He is reporting that a massive air and ground assault is taking place with overwhelming force. I sit back and I am thinking that the military can not wait to get into the fight the right way. Looking at the video footage from the report you can tell that the assault is a large-scale operation. There are so many explosions, the camera on the tripod is shaking during his live report. It is an impressive show of American military power. The Pentagon most likely had this planned many months ago, but never was given an okay to perform this assault. The reporter stated that he was told that soldiers would not be put in harms way on the ground. Instead they want to sterilize the ground, so we can avoid casualties. Our military is finally getting to concentrate on our soldiers first, instead of so-called civilians. War has many guarantees.

One guarantee of war is people die. No one is exempt from dieing. Casualties that are of innocent nature are so sad and useless. As with all activities of combat, many people claim to be innocent and are not. So whenever the military enters a conflict with an enemy that is not in uniform, it makes everyone a possible combatant. As a result, many truly innocent people, and our soldiers, are killed or injured. But the reality of war is the way you win is to kill the enemy, and unfortunately many civilians get caught up in the fight and die also. This fact must be figured into going to war and ending a war. Our leaders had made the decision many years ago to use nuclear weapons on Japan to end the war with Japan. Even though thousands lost their lives, it was, and still is believed, that the action of our government did save many more lives on both sides. In reality we had lost almost an entire generation of men. Most of the citizens of Japan had nothing and the quality of life was very poor. If the war continued the loss of life on the Japanese side would be horrific.

During my reflections the news reporter grabs his earpiece and says that he is told to clear the area. As he runs away from the fighting his cameraman holds the camera backwards facing the area of fighting. The picture went to a total whiteout for a second and I can see the largest non-nuclear explosion I have ever seen. After the initial explosion, I can see the heat wave coming from the area of the explosion. Neither the reporter nor I knew what this is, but it is a sign that our military is taking charge and have plans of ending this conflict on a grand scale.

As I sit and watch the events of the war as it unfolds, I am thinking about our society and different programs that are on in the evening. Americans have a love for television programs that deal with violence, crime, and law enforcement. When a program deals with theft, drugs, gang violence, or many of the different street crimes across the United States, I realize that most criminals were black men. I remember reading an article from the Boston Globe that stated that half the prison population was black men. The article continued to say that one in 10 black men would be in prison. I feel that somehow we have failed a race by not helping them prosper and so crime is what we got in return. Some believe the reason for the high numbers of incarcerated black men is because of the areas they live in. With areas of high crime, then more police patrols are required resulting in a higher arrest of black men. Anyway you look at it, we failed to get them into better areas and give them equal opportunities to prosper as the white population without prejudice. I once had a thought about helping with that situation.

In Israel, all young adults must serve a 2-year hitch in the military. This could be a good thing for us. I believe we should pass a law requiring all young adults at the age of 18 to spend time in the military. When I say all, I mean all. This includes the political children especially.

My theory behind this is very simple. All 18 year olds in the United States will go to boot camp, learn discipline, respect, a profession, and while doing so, can take college classes in their spare time. Now for those that do not graduate High School, they will be required to take classes in the military after basic training, to get them at the same level as the High School graduates. Once they complete this education then their time of 2 years starts from the completion of those educational classes. At that point everyone should be on equal terms.

Now my military is somewhat different than the present day military. Yes we need soldiers on the ground. But the military can also have trained troops that have a primary duty to provide services. By services I mean that we could have soldiers that do not march everyday, but provide essential services for those that do. In order to provide training for individuals that are interested in different career fields such as painting, construction, road maintenance, finance, medical, and many of the services that everyday civilian people perform, and the services that we hire independent private contractors for our military.

For those who have some disability, they still can function in the military. They can stay stateside and perform much-needed tasks such as clerical, technological, and so on. It would be better for all if we took a disabled person, if they are mentally capable, and give them a reason in life other than sitting around feeling sorry for themselves. Just because an individual has a physical problem does not mean that their mental capacity is not capable of performing certain tasks. This would put everyone on the same playing field. Also this would entitle some of them to receive much needed therapies and treatments, they may not be able to get in civilian life. By using someone that has a physical limitation that may not be able to get out and run in the desert, this frees up a more physically capable individual from sitting behind a desk, and enables he or she to perform as a soldier. The loss of a mind that a physical disabled individual has, is a tremendous loss to society. Usually when one has a disability, the other bodily functions are improved. It is like the brain has a required function, and if it is limited in one area, then it excels in other areas.

This will require our new Congress to do something they have not done in many years, and that is to perform the tasks they were appointed for. Be able to work out problems and enact legislation that does not have to do with some lobbyist handing them money. In many respects our new legislatures will be fun to watch.

What this new program would do is this. It would inspire the kids in school to make sure they are doing their best job learning as they can, because if they don't, they will understand that at 18, the military will pick them up, give them basic training, and they will have to take classes until the day they die, if they do not complete them properly. For those who only want to do their 2-year hitch, it is an incentive to make them perform early, and is to their advantage. This should create a reason for learning and becoming a partner in society. Now along with the military training and discipline they would be receiving, this would help them transform. For those who rebel against this idea, well they probably would wind up in prison anyway, and at least while off the streets they would not be terrorizing the public. This would put a real damper in the drug problem of the younger crowd, and as we all know when the demand is down, the money that is being spent on enforcement and confinement would also be saved to go to other needed programs. The ones who want to rebel and never have any intentions of making anything of their lives, they still will be part of the military. They will just have a different job. We could take these young Americans and confine them, but while in confinement they would still have to finish their schooling. Then we use them by performing tasks instead of sitting behind a concrete wall all day. I am not talking about hard labor, but perform functions that are useful. They could take the place of some of the construction and maintenance people that the government hires to do certain tasks. Such as they could perform lawn maintenance, painting, general cleanup and repair of facilities. If we are paying them to be in the military, then they should at least earn their keep. Now you say that some may not want to do the work. Well then how they perform and work will depend on their release back to the military for their 2-year hitch. Those people can learn and make something out of themselves. or they can rot. They will be the ones that will either rot there in the military or rot in some civilian prison. Since we are concerned with the money aspect then it would be cheaper to have them in military confinement with some usefulness, instead paying the outrageous cost of housing prisoners. What this does it makes the individual responsible for the outcome of their future. It is all their choice and not society. There will be some that will not conform and turn out useless, but it would save thousands of young kids from turning out rotten, and give them a sense of being. If you could put a mathematical pencil to this I can assure you that the amount of money that would be freed up would be great for our economy. It would also bring our military strength back to proper levels for our security.

That was only one idea that our little group had discussed. It would be an unpopular program at first, but in time it would show some great possibilities. This program would surely be classified as change, and many would not like this change either. But this program would have a positive outcome.

I remember when children grew up and were taught respect. I personally feel that our children made the turn to corruption when punishment was taken out of the schools. The teachers lost control of the kids. It all boiled down to mathematics. Children were spending more time with their teachers than their parents. The more time that they spent causing trouble and doing as they pleased, would overtake the time they spent with their parents. Naturally with pressure from the other kids to rebel, perform illegal activities, and the lack of quality time from parents, we ended up with an uneducated, rude, and rebellious generation of spoiled brats. Our government response was to protect those future voters. Giving rights to those who have not earned them as quality members of society has produced thousands of worthless, lazy individuals that believe that everyone owes them a living. I was really looking forward to ending the welfare system and putting these fat ass people to work instead of watching Oprah or the View all day. But that was only my opinion.

I was thinking by the time all of this change was to take effect, and we had a newly elected and functional government again, I may not be alive to see it all happen. We all were hoping for a speedy recovery, but it would not come about over night. Our best weapon was energetic people with a desire to return America to the great nation it once was. But we had to take this at one day at a time.

It is time I should head for bed. When I get tired my mind wanders in many directions. This is one time that I need to stay focused on what is about to happen. Tomorrow at this time I will either be celebrating or locked up somewhere. Either way I have made my bed and I will gladly sleep in it.

CHAPTER 7

▼

THE DAY HAS COME

After a rough night trying to get some sleep, I was woke up again by the sound of a bugle. Traditional military still uses a horn to wake you. It is 0530 hours, and the day is sure to be long, and hopefully successful. I get up and open my door to see people milling around the area, but the noise level was way low. It is a day of serious thought and execution. It is the morning of a day that I have pushed the right buttons to create. I am really nervous and scared. What I need is a good cup of coffee. So I hurry, get dressed, and ready for the day. I head toward the food tent.

As I arrived at the tent, there is a large crowd of people having coffee, and only a few eating breakfast. Most of them looked like I feel from having a hard night. Any other day there would be loud talking and laughter. Today is different. People are talking low, and there is a more serious atmosphere than usual. The military personnel are the only ones acting like a normal day. As I look around, Lt. Johnson caught my eye and waved to me, as his tank crew head out of the tent to prepare for a busy day. This is the first time I have seen all of his crew together away from the tank. Usually one member stays behind to provide security for the tank.

I get up to get another cup of coffee and I notice there is another military truck parked besides the tank. There are military police watching the tank and some soldiers are unloading a couple of military police vehicles. One has a .50 caliber Browning machine gun mounted on top of it. That has drawn a small crowd of people to see what is going on. As I approach the tank, a military fuel truck pulls up to the truck hauling the tank, and back up to refuel the tank. It has not run that much but I have been told the fuel mileage is not real good on that piece of equipment. A military police officer tells everyone to stay away from the area so they can do their job. So I watch from a distance. All of these men and women are armed and I assumed they have ammunition. I am sure that some do, because the man in charge of the .50 caliber has loaded a belt of ammunition in the weapon, and from my limited view it looks like it is ready in case it is needed.

I have a half an hour before our morning meeting, so I just walk around and watch everyone. It is interesting watching different people, and how they are handling the day we have been working for. Some are very somber, some are coming alive and starting to relax more, and then there are a few that are really pumped up. Those are the people that concern me. This operation requires a calm approach. The last thing I want to happen is the formation of a mob mentality. As I start to walk toward our meeting place, I notice some buses are pulling in, to start taking people to the staging areas closer to Washington. I am worried about the people that have to wait a few hours before we start our operation. Too much idle time can be dangerous.

As I enter the tent, I have the feeling the military is taking on a larger role than what I had thought yesterday. The tent is half full of high-ranking officers from Captains to Admirals. They have armed guards with them for their protection. There is a tripod that is covered with something fairly large on it. Most of the officers are wearing shoulder holsters. There are four military police officers there and they have two German Shepard dogs with them. The dogs are sitting beside their handlers, but they do not look very enthused with the activities. There is a buffet line with four tables and chairs for all of us to sit at. In here food does not seem like a very big priority, but the coffee pot is getting quite a bit of attention. One of the Captains' walk to the podium and say, "Gentlemen you might want to eat something. This will be the last hot meal for today."

After a few more minutes the same Captain again approaches the podium. Everyone got quiet and became attentive. He looks around and says, "Well this is a day that I never thought would happen here in America. But we all feel that if something drastic is not done very quickly, the security of our country can be jeopardized, and I personally do not want to have to learn Arabic or Chinese. The military branches of the United States are totally involved in the operation. We actually are going to do our duty and protect the citizens, leadership, and the establishment of our government. We held back to see how much public support there would be, and also to get needed civilian ideas and information. The support that you have assembled is overwhelming. It has been so great that we have decided to take over control of the action. For security reasons, and operational control, the members of the parade will not be allowed to have live ammunition with them, or in their weapons. The reason you needed armed supporters were mainly because of the military, and the different law enforcement agencies that may have confronted you. It is safe to say that you do not need arms against us. And we will handle the other agencies to include the Secret Service." As he looked over to Admiral Wilson he says, "The Admiral will be in overall charge of the operation. He has a few things to say."

Well this is a shock to see that we will be involved in part with a military coup. Or is this just a ploy to overpower us? This is a legitimate thought. Every camp, or staging area, has a large piece of military equipment parked there. If they all are like our camp, there are many armed military soldiers in the camp. This can very possibly be a way to stop our operation. So before the Admiral gets to the podium I jump up and say, "Excuse me Captain. This change in policy is greatly needed and appreciated, but at the same time it looks like we are going to be the ones taken over, and not our government." The Captain smiled and said, "This is why Admiral Wilson is here. He will explain everything."

The Admiral approached the podium, looked around, and said, "Well everyone, here we are. To answer your question is simple. It was not but a few days ago that we agreed to participate in this endeavor. We have heard rumors of this and most of you were under surveillance. It was not until we were able to confirm that your major concern was the security of America, that is when we decided to become involved. Since the Joint Chiefs have no knowledge of who from the military is involved, we have taken our own steps, but we kept the option open to either disperse this group of people or take over. We decided to take over, but with your help. For over two hundred years our country was strong, and there was pride in the leadership. Now it has turned to personal gain. America is headed for self-destruction unless we fix it. And the only way that we will fix it, is to get rid of our current leadership. In a way it is a sad day. But on the other hand, it is a new beginning for America."

While the Admiral fumbles through his notes, I look around, and everyone in the room is in a daze. We all are looking at each other, and then the Admiral said, "It is imperative that this action has the appearance that the population of America organized, planned, and initiated this coup. The American people will not like a military take over, but when the citizens do it, well the plan will be easier to sell. The other little item that we will need is, one of you will need to confront the President, and let him know that the citizens of the United States have fired him, and not the military. As we speak James Lucas is having a meeting with the members of the Supreme Court. We just heard a few minutes ago that the Supreme Court privately said, that the Constitution and the Declaration of Independence did have provisions, for the citizens to over throw rouge or corrupt administrations, and Congress, that is dangerous to our security. Once we got the so-called blessing from the Supreme Court, we can now confront the President, and all members of the leadership. With this blessing, or opinion, the military can aid the citizens. Actually this gives us the right to control this situation. With the opinion of the highest legal court of this great land, no one here can be prosecuted, unless they commit an act of violence or illegal activity. This gives us the authorization to call for martial law. I now would like General Davis to provide you with more details, but I would like to say to all of you, Thank you. Thank you for being so concerned for our country that you would sacrifice your safety, and your family's safety, to do what you feel is right. This time let us make the right choices at the voting booth so we do not have to do this again." And Admiral Wilson got a round of applause and walked out of the tent.

General Davis stood to the side of the podium and says, "Three weeks ago I was planning on retiring. Admiral Wilson called me and said he had gotten word about a take over of Washington D.C. This I had to see this myself. Now since the court has said that it is legal and just with our operation, many things have changed. I will be the man in charge on the ground here in Washington. The times and schedules that you were briefed on yesterday will still be in effect, with a few little changes. The parade and re-enactments at the mall will still go on. But, there will be only powder rounds used and no bullets or balls will be allowed. You are concerned that no one will get hurt. That is why we will take over the physical nature of this mission, and most people will not see anything. We are going to shut down Washington D.C., and anyone that wants to leave, can leave. Only cleared personnel will be allowed to enter the city. The military police guard unit from Florida is on the way to Andrews Air Force Base. They will patrol the streets of Washington, along with the Washington Police, and there will be zero tolerance on the curfews. The staging area at Fort Stanton Park is being converted into a tent city for violators. It will also be a housing area for some suspected terrorist and other bad people, we have wanted to apprehend, but the administration would not let us. Security is job one with this mission. If all goes well, within seventy two hours this will all be over, and we should be able to lift the martial law status and let the country get back to normal. It only took 100 hours to take Iraq down in the first Gulf War, so 72 hours should give us plenty of time to perform our duties. The hard work will be after this is over. You seem to have the majority of the issues concerning the economy and legislation under control for now. We can help some with these issues, but it will be important that we get some solid civilian leadership back in power as soon as we can. The longer there is no leadership in the White

House, the more it will look like the military has taken over, which is against our Constitution. However, with the Supreme Courts opinion, we do now have the right to take charge. At 1300 hours we will all travel in a civilian convoy to the Capitol building, where we will inform everyone there, they need to find a new job. Capitol Security and the Park police have already been taken care of. We will have no resistance. However, unless a designated individual escorts someone, there will absolutely be no one allowed to enter a federal building. The people in this room will be escorted into the White House for a brief visit, but you will not be allowed in the security areas at this time. I do want to stress this to you. By 1400 hours today our country will be more secure than it has ever been. The Guard units from California, Texas, Arizona and New Mexico were deployed on the border last night. No one will get into the United States from that border alive. The northern border with Canada is being monitored in those areas that we know have had an issue with illegal border crossings. Most of those have been drug and weapons smugglers, and not terrorists. The CIA and other agencies, have been alerted, and are in full swing with the largest information gathering operation that the world has ever seen. Israel is providing us with very detailed information from the Mid East areas. The relations with Israel have been damaged, but we will get that relationship back on track shortly. Does anyone have any questions at this time?"

The hands fly up, and General Davis calls on one of our people, that is working with the security issues. His name is Jack Lemmon. Jack asks, "What will happen to those from Mexico that try to cross the border?" The General replies, "They will be searched, stripped of everything they have, and taken to the nearest border crossing. Each one will be issued an order like a no trespassing order, and this order tells them that if they attempt to cross the border again, they could be locked up indefinitely without representation, in a hellhole of a facility." Jack asks, "What happens if Mexico refuses to take the detainees?" The General smiles and says, "Mexico is more screwed up economically, and has more corruption than we do. The one thing they rely on is the money, the U.S. gives them for aid every year, and our purchase of oil. The money and the flow of oil will cease if we have any problems. We have had some high level meetings with members of the Mexican government in the past ,and we have agreed to help them with the drug problems. The CIA is going to be in the lead with that effort, but the military will also be involved. Not being able to smuggle their drugs into the United States is going to hurt the Cartels fairly rapidly. Trying to take on our military at the border will end their campaign even more rapidly."

Dan Martin, who has been heading up our committee on economics asks, "What happens to all of the illegal aliens that are already here?" The

General says, "That is going to be an issue for the new administration. We will deal with security at home and abroad, but the civilians will have to determine what to do about that situation. The military presence on the streets of America is not a picture that we want seen around the world. The other agencies that I described earlier, included Immigration agencies, will be looking for unwanted individuals. They will track them down and get rid of them. We can still perform missions on the ground in the United States while we are under a limited version of martial law." Dan asks the General, "Do you see major problems from other countries?" General Davis replies, "One of the reasons we decided to participate in your mission was we are going to be granted complete security decisions and actions, of the wars we currently have ongoing. With the past and present administrations, we have been limited so much by politics, most of our loss of life has been from some policy limiting our responses to threats against our troops. Many of you are veterans of the military, and we are thankful that you see the importance of our running the security to get it where it should be. Since the security and war effort has been temporarily turned over to us for a short period of time, the ground will shake in some of those countries. We are not politicians, we are warriors. My primary duty to my country is to secure the United States, and prevent war. But when our civilian leaders get us into a war, it is my job to end it as swiftly and efficiently as I can. We, at the Pentagon, all hate the loss of life no matter who it is, We are here to protect our citizens first, even before our allies. If I have to drop a MOAB (Mother of all Bombs) that kill many, to save our soldiers, I will issue the order and give a prayer for those that are about to receive this terrible weapon. If any of you got a chance to see the news report from Afghanistan last night, you may have noticed that we have already ramped up the activities. We figure that it will take you a little longer than what you think to get everything ready for a new election of officials to take over our government. We feel that six months to a year is a good estimate. That means we have a short time to end this bloody battle that rages in the Middle East. None of us have any political desires, and we do not care who we piss off. If the Arabs try and use oil as leverage, then they can shove it. We have many countries, that would love to sell their oil to us at a cheaper price. The military is like a business. The difference is that we do not make money but we can do a lot to limit expenditures. This is not a pleasant subject but lets us look at the expense of a death of a soldier, verses a soldier that looses a limb from a roadside bomb. When a soldier dies we issue the beneficiary a check for fifty thousand dollars. We have the expense of a military funeral, which is not that much. When a soldier is injured and looses a leg, that expense raises to almost half a million, and sometimes even more. So to run a business properly we have to get rid of the bombs. You will see a decline in roadside bombs, because the people placing these bombs have been off limits. For some reason our politicians have protected them so someone would not get pissed at us. Well as of tomorrow it is going to be a pissing match. We have multiple places where bomb making materials have been stored, and we know of many safe houses that assemble these bombs. Tomorrow there will be many that will die that make these bombs. No bombs, no injured soldiers and civilians, mean less money spent. Good business. I am not for sure what our new leaders will choose to do, but in the mean time while we have your blessing on securing our people and our country, we are going to eliminate multiple threats. Those people and nations that think they can hurt us through terrorism and other means, will have a new sense of urgency to go and pick on someone else. Also, by the end of the week the farmers of Afghanistan will be planting corn, because there will be no more poppy fields."

The General continues, "You folks have to realize something. In a political situation, it sometimes is beneficial for our leaders to have a large, unpopular casualty number, to support their agenda. That is one of the reasons why we have had our hands tied with offensive missions. Our job for the past couple of years has been trying to keep our soldiers alive, under unfavorable conditions and limitations. This has now ceased. We will change from a defensive position to a very aggressive offensive force, that has not been seen since the first Gulf War".

It is my time to ask another question. "General what about these other countries that are always threatening our every move?" "Well Russia is not a problem. They have watched for decades their war machines being defeated by the United States in war with other countries. What do you think that is in the mind of some young tank driver in Russia that hears that they will face an Abrams tank, and the A-10 Warthog? I guarantee you that many will run like hell, and the fight will not last long. Iran is really a messed up country. We are trying to train some of their people to manage a government and do away with the current Islamic law, that punishes their own people. The country of Iran is almost out of basic essentials, and most of the country is out of fresh water and electricity. Those areas where they have electricity, is because we want them to have it. North Korea is almost history. Their leader just won't die, but the people of that country are tired of being starved. They are ready for their own revolution, and I would say within the next couple of years, the two Korea's will be one again, under a democratic society. We will streamline that time some in the next couple of months. Pakistan has already been alerted to pull their troops out away from the border of Afghanistan and Pakistan. In a few days that area will be a sinkhole. Bin Laden will get to see his 72 virgins. He will see them in Hell."

Before the General could say anything else, the sound of a chopper was heard, and he told us it was time to go. We all got up and headed outside. Now that we are leaving, I am hungry. What poor timing. But like a good little soldier I head out the door, after grabbing a couple of biscuits. The Admiral and the General got on board the chopper and flew off. We all got into different SUV's and took off to the Capitol. Most of the people that stayed at our facility, have already been taken to their places of duty by bus, while we were inside. Mainly they will be a photo opportunity for the rest of the country to see. Their voice will be more powerful then the weapons. Even though I had just listened to a briefing of what procedures are about to happen, I still have no idea, what is about to happen.

I pictured wide spread fighting with the common people that are in Washington D.C. at the time of our actions. I hope this will not be the case, but I do not know exactly what to expect. Even though we have been informed regularly on how things are going, I am not aware of the role that the military has taken, and how much they have done to make this happen in a non-violent way. When someone pictures military involvement of this nature, it usually reminds me of the scene of Kent State University, when the National Guard shot several people. I have a vision of military soldiers, armed, having to fight their way through the streets that are filled with tear gas. I can picture water cannons being used on crowds, and some trying to take advantage, and have large-scale riots and looting. This however, is not the case. As we drive through the streets of the Capital, most people do not have any idea of anything going on. It looks calm and people are watching all the Civil War activities, and not paying any attention to the presence of a large number of present day soldiers. One thing that I do know, if we were entirely in control of this venture, the outcome might not be so calm. Our military has once again shown us that they too believe the best means to an end is non-violent. But we have also just started the coup.

We arrived at the Capitol at 1300 hours, and entered the Capitol building. What a magnificent place this is. The Speaker of the House met us as we entered. She is truly a witch. She tried to tell us that we would all wind up in jail, but as she yelled at one of the military officers, she leaned forward and tried to slap him. Immediately the military police, that was with us, slammed her to the floor, handcuffed her, and marched her out of the building. At that time General Davis entered and says, "She can be the first visitor to go to Fort Stanton. And for your information Madam, the Supreme Court ruled that our actions are just." And with that she is taken out of the building. The General turned and says, "Can you believe that she was third in line for the Presidency. We were worried that she would have the President and Vice-President assassinated, so she could take over. That would be a cold day in hell before we would let that happen. She was one of the considerations, that help sway our opinion for this operation. We were deeply concerned with her, her beliefs, and actions."

There are only a few politicians and a few aides in the building. They are shocked to hear that they have lost their job. Some are swearing and some are crying. But the one thing they have been told is that it is the citizen's of the United States that orchestrated this, and not the military. Everyone is escorted out of the building, and the Capitol Police secured the building. The Capital police have been briefed earlier and knew what to expect only a few minutes before we arrived. General Davis turned to us and says, "It is time to tour the White House." We left the building by a back entrance and drove over to the White House. There is military police with the security at the White House, and we can see concerned Secret Service Agents standing outside on the lawn of the White House. As we enter the building one of the agents ask us to respect the White House. I said to him, "The reason that we have done what we are doing is to preserve this house as well as yours. How do you listen to these criminals talk about cheating the average American and you ignore it?" He replies, "My job does not concern me with conversations. I protect the President." I looked at him laughing, "Well it appears at this time in your career, you failed to live up to your expectations. He is right along with the other eight million American people that are out of work. However you still have your job."

We got the average tour that most American tourist get when they go to Washington D.C. and see the White House. We got the VIP tour because General Davis is a historian that knows all of the history of the White House. The entrance is amazing. It is lined with portraits of past presidents, and artifacts that continued to the Cross Hall. The East Room is a very large room that once was used as a laundry room by First Lady Abigail Adams. The room mainly remained in shambles after the fire of 1814 and was finally restored by Theodore Roosevelt. In the center of the State Floor of the White House is the Blue room. The presidents are able to receive guest using this room. I feel the reason is because it has a great view of the South Lawn.

The Green Room has some unique history. This room is where President Madison signed the declaration of war on the British in 1812. The British came back in 1814 and set the Green Room on fire, as well as most of the White House. General Davis states, "We will not let anyone use this time to inflict damage to this building, or any other federal building. This too is a reason why we chose to take more control of this mission. We cannot take a chance someone will attempt to make a statement by doing damage to our infrastructure."

We did get to see the swimming pool, the pressroom, some other important rooms, and finally in the West Wing, we see the Oval Office. We are told to not enter, but we can look as long as we want to. It really is an awesome sight. It is a sight that I will remember for the rest of my life. One of our members made the comment that he was glad that President Bush had the carpet changed after Bill and Monica. From the Cabinet Room and Oval Office you have a good view of the famous Rose Garden. The Oval Office is located in the Center of the West Wing. It is connected to both the Cabinet Room and the Chief of Staff's Office. I have often wondered who really is in charge. The President or the Chief of Staff.

It is 1630 hours and we received a report that all commercial and civilian aircraft are on the ground, except for two overseas flights that are being escorted by Navy fighters. The borders are secured and I have not heard one shot. Martial Law has been declared for the whole country except for Alaska, Hawaii, and Puerto Rico. Our next stop is the Pentagon. At 1745 hours we arrive at the Pentagon. A massive and actually unimpressive building when you are up close to it. Seeing it from the air, in the normal pictures, the Pentagon is different than standing in front of it. Or is there a front? One of the reasons that we are glad that the military does need our presence at the Pentagon is it is not actually located in Washington D.C. It is located in Virginia. General Davis personally walks us down numerous halls. We arrive at a room set up like a classroom, and many of the other members and people I have seen are here. In the room there is a map of the United States with a few red dots on them. We are told they are military aircraft flying over the country in a show of support. One has a blue arrow through it, and I am told that it is what we know as Air Force One, giving the President and his family their final flight to Chicago. It is reported that he is very upset. The thought of loosing all of that money from the lobbyist is almost too much for him to bear. And how will he explain this to his children? The rest of the country knows how it feels to be punished for no reason by the administration, so his children will have to learn to live with it. Unfortunately it is always the innocent that bears the burden of the corrupt.

We are briefed that most of the states said they will comply with our policies. They have no choice or they will have no money to operate either. During the initial broadcast it is made clear to the country, and explained, that if the states do not comply with help during this matter of security, the federal government will take all land and sell it. That got the citizens of each state demanding that their individual state comply. Just the thought of mass eminent domain is a scary scenario. And the public and states still have no idea of what kind of threat the United States has come under. I can see how easy it is to be so powerful that with a few words the civilians of a state get off their butt and stand up for their Constitutional rights. This plan was not drawn up by the military but our planners. I watch this scenario play out with a state being arrogant and defiant, and then with only a few words concerning money and land, the attitude turns into submission. All the leaders of the states are concerned their life, as they currently know it, may be over also. The country seems to be fired up. We are briefed over some other situations, and we are told that we actually will meet in one of the meeting rooms at the Capitol. The White House will be secured for the new administration. But after a day of no one dying from a bullet, I feel good. The military has reserved us rooms at some fancy hotel, so I wander off with the rest of the folks, and get on the bus to my new temporary home. I need a drink but during this martial law alcohol sales are prohibited. Upon arriving at the hotel we are all given rooms that are already designated. When I get to my room I am surprised that all of my gear is here. Even my smuggled bottle I have brought with me has been gathered and placed in my bag. The bummer is that there is only one television station on, and that one is an information station explaining what is going on, and warning people to stay in their homes, unless they have to work, or if they are having an emergency. I go out of the room and buy a Coke and come back in and mix me a drink. I walk over to the balcony and look down to the city. We are on the sixth floor and the streets are abandoned. No one is on the streets except for armed military police and the Washington police. The sight of the lack of people is such a change from the city a few hours earlier. During the day the streets are full of tourists. I wonder where they all have gone. In the distance, I can see many places where emergency vehicle lights are flashing. I cannot tell what is happening.

I am able to take a long hot shower, and between that and the drink, I finally am relaxed. I can go to sleep and sleep for a couple of days. But that is not in the cards. Someone is knocking at the door. I get up with only my pants on and answered the door. Standing here is two military policemen and a Marine Captain. The Captain identifies himself as from Naval Intelligence from the Pentagon. He informs me that General Davis has told him I am the liaison between the military and the new civilian leadership. It would have been a nice thing for someone to tell me of my new appointment. The reason he is here is to escort me back to the Pentagon concerning a foreign matter. Now my ability to conduct foreign affairs is most likely not what our country will have in mind. I do not understand the political arena. But what am I going to say? I hurry and get dressed and down the elevator I go to an awaiting SUV. There are two plain-clothes people in the front seat, and we take off like a bat out of hell. We are not too far from the Pentagon and it only takes about ten minutes to get there. The trip there is strange. We are the only vehicles on the road at this time. As we drive down the road, patrols of soldiers are seen walking the streets of Washington D.C..

The Captain escorts me into the building to the first security desk where I get a security badge and place it on my shirt. We walk down some of the same hallways that I did earlier in the day but we take a different turn. This hall has four security check points. At the end of the hall is a door that almost looks like a safe. It is only lacking the combination lock and the handle to open the door. It seems to open and close by little electric actuators. When the door opens I almost fell over. It is a room that is filled with large screens of maps and video monitors. General Davis and Admiral Wilson are there and General Davis motioned for me to come over to him.

I went over to General Davis and he points to a television with a view of a ship in the distance. He says, "We were wrong about North Korea. One of our Navy patrol boats is in international waters. Two boats similar to our World War II PT boats attacked them. Two torpedoes were fired from these boats. One missed the Navy ship and the other hit the stern of the ship damaging the rudder. They are unable to turn away and leave. The attack boats came from this vessel, which is an older Navy ship they bought from France." He is pointing at the ship that is on the television screen. He looks at me and asks, "If you are in charge right now what would you do?" I came right back at him with a reply, "I would blow that ship out of the water. I don't mean hit it where it might sink over a period of time but hit it with overkill." Admiral Wilson asks, "Why would you do that?" My reply, "This way any other nation that wants to play will think twice before attacking. They have all been warned that we will not tolerate an act of violence during this transition. It will be the right time to show everyone that the United States is back and our word is gospel and shall be respected." The General and the Admiral looks at each other and Admiral Wilson says, "We wanted to get your opinion on this matter. I wanted to see how serious you are about national security. You have passed the test and we will attack this ship in a matter of minutes. We have a carrier that is about two hundred miles away and they have launched four planes. They will attack that ship and do precisely as you said, if North Korea refuses to back off, so we can tow our ship out of the area. Just because we are the most powerful nation, we are also compassionate. I will give them a chance to leave. A very quick chance."

At this time, our crippled ship sent a message to the Joint Chiefs that the smaller attack boats are heading toward the ship again. This time the rooms lit up like a Kiss concert. People are busy and then over a speaker we could hear the pilots of the F-18's, being given clearance to fire upon all ships in the area. The pilots are in radio contact with the ship. The pilot told the ship that his squadron would strike the two attack boats, and then the mother ship. They want to coordinate their fire so our Navy ship will not shoot one of our planes down. As the first plane headed toward the first attack boat we can hear the pilot say, "You picked the wrong day to screw with us." After that we can see tracers hitting the small boat and then it exploded and almost immediately sank. The second plane aimed at the other small boat, which is turning around to head back to the mother ship. It too has a violent end to its' life. As soon as the second attack boat went up in smoke the mother ship exploded so violently, the entire structure above the deck just disappears. After a few more seconds another explosion is seen and the ship starts sinking slowly at the bow. While we watch the men jumped off of the ship into the water, another explosion, that has twice the power of the first one, hit the ship. When the smoke and fire clear all that is left is burning debris on the surface of the water. The ship is gone. Then we can hear one of the pilots tell our ship that they will hang around for a while, in case some one else wants to come and play. The Captain of the Navy vessel told the pilots that he did not know who are running this situation, but whoever it is has his vote. The Admiral looks at me and says, "You have your first voter." I reply, "No way in hell Admiral. I am not planning on being a politician. What happened here is what should have happened. North Korea picked the fight and they lost. I would show that video all over the world so all the nations know that we mean business. And I would definitely show our people this video to let them know security is number one here, and then we will deal with the other issues." In reality North Korea may have done us a very big favor. This is the first time that I can remember since the Vietnam War where other ships, and not terrorists, attacked a U.S. Navy ship. We have done nothing wrong. We were attacked. We warned the stupid leaders of North Korea, and they made their decision, and the price has been paid. I looked at General Davis and ask, "Well what else has went on?" He says, "So far we lost a couple of soldiers in Los Angeles. Hispanic gangs tried to take on our units that are aiding the police enforce martial law. Evidentially, they were unable to meet with their suppliers across the border, and tried to take it out on law enforcement. A Cobra that is aiding the border security personnel flew in, and ripped them a new ass. As the Cobra approached small arms fire came from the crowd from everywhere, and he opened up with all he had. The number of casualties is not known for sure, but it is high. A couple of politicians committed suicide, which is no loss. We have detained a large number of illegal border crossers, and the border patrol said that they recovered a large amount of drugs. Surveillance shows that most of the people approaching the border has hunkered down or turned back. The Coast Guard has seized many ships with immigrants trying to get to our coast. Some have drugs on them, and some have explosives and weapons. We had two planes that attempted to fly under the radar and were forced down. One had to be fired upon to get his attention. They both have been apprehended. We had a tank at one of our checkpoints chase down a car and force it off of the road. The individual wanted to get home, and in her mind the United States military was not going to keep her from reaching her destination. She was transferred to Fort Stanton and she is having a fit. To clear the road the tank pushed her new Jaguar into the river. She suffered some injuries, nothing bad."

Okay so far it has not been that bad. We have gangs rioting in L.A., which is normal. The loss of two soldiers is very sad. Then, a couple of pilots trying to sneak home. Immigrants trying to get to the promise land, and a dumb bitch tried to take on an Abrams tank. If that is all that happens the first night, we have done well. As far as the foreign relations department, we showed diplomacy is not a thing that we have time for right now. We will need to get someone that has the patience for negotiations. As I stand in this room, with the finest technology available, I can tell this is not any time to play games. As far as I am concerned, the military can do exactly what they did with North Korea, if a threat is imminent. The only difference is that the bigger the threat the larger the bomb. As usual the United States military has successfully done their job, when they were left alone and not interfered with. North Korea has played their hand and lost the game. The sad part of this for me is that in my celebration of no one getting hurt from our side, we did loose two soldiers. That is two too many.

At this time the Admiral gets a phone call. He tells whoever that is on the other end of the phone line, "Let North Korea know that attacking our ship in international waters is an act of war. And since the military is currently in charge of security for our country, and we do not have a civilian process to go through, they may not want to try another stupid venture. If they do the response will be quick, but it will not last very long." He looks over to me and I say, "That sounds like good diplomacy to me Admiral, but what do you mean by not lasting too long?" He replies, "With that answer it may appear that we are talking nuclear. It will not take a nuclear bomb to wipe out North Korea's will to fight. This will make China and Russia add a lot of pressure on North Korea to stand down. I doubt if we hear from North Korea any time soon."

General Davis tells me that we have a meeting planned in the morning at the Capitol building with some other important individuals and they would like for me to attend. I agree but tell him that I really do not have much to wear. He tells me I will be taken in the morning to go shopping to find some suitable clothes for the meeting. That does not leave me with much time for sleep but I can't complain. I am free and unharmed. We have completed our mission and now we have to figure out what we are to do next.

On the way back to the hotel it finally hit me. I was just part of a take over of the most powerful country in the world, and I did nothing. It was just like a drive downtown. The military, and the other people involved, have done everything, and I am on a sight seeing tour. The streets of Washington D.C. has an eerie feeling to them. With the exception of the security details the streets are quiet. Lights are on in many buildings but it is like no one is home. The Capitol and White House at night are lit up, and it is a beautiful picture. We come across a couple of men being arrested by the local police and the military for violating the curfew. Other than this it is a dead town.

The next morning I wake up at six o'clock, order breakfast, and a pot of coffee from room service. While I am having a good cup of coffee, I receive a call notifying me that I will be picked up at seven thirty, to be taken on a shopping trip. How fun. I hate shopping. But I hurry, get a shower, and put on some clothes. I get a call telling me that the car is five minutes out and to meet them downstairs. I go to the elevator and down I go. As soon as I get downstairs, the big, black SUV pulls up, and a man gets out and opens the back door for me. I get in and off we go to a large clothing store. There I am again met by a man who takes me into the part of the store, where there are all kinds of suits and sport jackets. I hate ties and I was told that slacks and a sport jacket will be suitable for what we are doing. So, after a quick measurement, off I go into the dressing room with an arm full of clothes. With the assistance of the salesman, we pick out a couple of sets of clothing and some shoes, so I will look presentable. I get dressed and off we go to the Capitol building. Again very few people are on the street, and the town looks necked without the tourist. It was one of the few nights in Washington D.C. that some murder had not been committed. I can be happy with that also.

As we are driving toward the capitol building I am able to get a good view of Washington D. C. that I would have never seen with people on the streets. The town is in desperate need of repair. This city should be an example of how great America is and how we take care of things in our country. But instead what I see is a city that looks like it is in poverty. Why do our leaders let the Capitol of America get in this terrible shape? With all of the historical and precious sites that are in this town I cannot believe that our leaders let this place go to hell. I imagine that Washington D. C. did not get any stimulus money. Out of all of the wasteful spending this would have been a good place to do some needed renovations. Looking at this city justified what we are doing is good. Greed has made people blind. The majority of our Capitol is in shambles. Other than the federal buildings, this place needs a bulldozer to flatten everything and start over. The closer we get to the Capitol, the more traffic I see heading in the same direction as we are.

When we get about two blocks from the Capitol we come upon a military checkpoint. There are plenty of armed soldiers. As we pull up to the checkpoint one of the men that is with us, handed them some papers, and they let us in. Then one man turned to me and says, "This identification card you must have on your person at all times." I took the card and it has a photo of me, from where I do not know. I clip it on my shirt. As we pull up in the rear of the Capitol, the men in the front seat get out and open the door. One opens the back of the SUV and pulls out a metal briefcase, and hands it to me. He says, "This is for you." I take it and head toward the door.

I am escorted into the building and I am surprised to see a large gathering of people. We are being escorted to the room where the Speaker of the House controls the House of Representatives. In here I notice some of the former politicians and the entire membership of the Supreme Court. The Joint Chiefs represents the military, and with them are many aides. James Lucas is sitting at the head of the bench where the Speaker of the House used to sit. I am being directed to the front row, where many of our original members are also sitting. I have a very strange feeling being in this room. James welcomes everyone and it is so quiet you can hear a pin drop.

James opens the meeting by saying, "I welcome everyone here today to be a part of the New United States of America. How our country turns out in the future is going to be determined by your decisions here today and in days to come. A few long months ago a few of our original members got the idea of a coup from listening to the general public. As you all are aware this room became a place of business, and not in the best interest of the citizens of America. It was being turned into a backroom, where private deals were being put together, and the outcome of these deals were how much money each member of the legislature could make. This type of business was a daily operation of members of government, that decided they would take advantage of the citizens of our country. Well that business is now over. What the people do to these elected criminals will be determined by the new administration, when the public elects them. We are here to determine policy that we will implement in the absence of a permanent government. Our first order of business is the security of the United States. For those of you that have not heard, North Korea attacked one of our ships in international waters last night, after they had received the news of our change of government. Our security has been turned over to the military without civilian interference, temporarily. The Joints Chief of Staff took control over the situation and eliminated the threat. Later on we will show you the video of the military action against the aggressors. At this time I would like General Davis to come up and fill you in on our military situation at this time."

General Davis approaches the bench and stands in front of James and says, "Good morning everyone. It has been a busy week for us in the military, as with many of you. I want to fill you in on the role of the U. S. Military. Presently we have full control of our nuclear arsenal. All weapons are secure and all personnel are in place as usual. We are on a general alert level within the military, and a raised level of alert with South Korea. At this time we have not heard from North Korea concerning last nights incident, but we will be ready for anything. We currently have a massive intelligence-gathering mission in operation all around the world. Most of our allies have joined us in this information-gathering mission. The video of last nights attack has been sent out to many countries to show them that we are fully operational, and at this time we have limited patience with stupidity. Our borders are currently being secured by our military, using the most aggressive campaign ever seen to keep unwanted individuals out of our country. Our Navy and Air Force are actively patrolling the oceans around the United States. At the present time, no outside aircraft are allowed to enter our airspace. No ships, without inspections, are allowed in our territorial waters. If you are planning on a vacation in Europe in the next few days, you can forget about it. Nothing is going in or out without our authorization. With the help of the Reserve units, our Homeland Security is inspecting every shipping container coming off ship onto shore. The FBI is currently working on picking up certain individuals that appear to be an internal threat to our security. Martial law gives us greater power to do certain things. We are not going to overstep our powers and abuse people. All agencies will adhere as closely to the law as they can. But when there is good reason, then we will search, or pursue individuals and places, as we deem necessary. Steve Taylor sitting up front on the end here will be the liaison between the Pentagon and you. We forgot to inform him of his new job yesterday, so he had quite a surprise last night. He will be briefed at least once a day, and will keep you informed on what is going on. If you have suggestions concerning our activity or manner of execution, give them to Steve and we will look at every one of them. We are a democracy. But we are going to turn up the heat on the war effort. No one is hearing a peep out of Iran. After sinking the North Korean ships, we feel that Iran is not going to rock the boat for now. We are increasing our presence of being seen more in Iraq. Reminding people that we are still there. Afghanistan is no longer a political issue, and we have given our orders to Pakistan. They have been part of the problem, but they will become part of the solution in a couple of days. We have already started the most aggressive offensive in Afghanistan, the United States military has engaged in since the Korean War. The world will shake for a few minutes in a couple of days and hopefully, Afghanistan will no longer be a big problem. We might be better off giving her to Russia. They seem to want that damn desert for some reason, so maybe a good faith gift would help relations."

Laughing was heard all through this large room. That comment seemed to relax everyone and made them more comfortable. Even General Davis cracked a smile. After a short pause, General Davis says, "The security of our nation is the easy part for you at this time. We are dealing with it. The other issues that are part of running a country, is the work that is ahead of you. We will keep you informed, and we ask the same from you. We will keep you posted through Steve on matters that we are dealing with. Don't be surprised if the military happens to ask your advice from time to time. To do this right, and put our country back on top will take all of us working together. I will have more detailed information later in the day. You gentlemen have a good day." And the General walked down and sat down.

James and one of the members of the Attorney General's office came to the microphone. James says, "Since the Supreme Court ruled in our favor so to speak, we wanted them here to see, and advise us in getting this country back on track. As you know we have a lot of work ahead of us. The Supreme Court will assist us on enforcing the mandates of our Constitution, to insure we do it properly. Later on we will discuss and vote on an individual, that will speak to the people for us. There have been several suggestions. Our issue that faces us is simple. We would like to leave as many people that work for the federal agencies on the job. They not only have the expertise in their field, but also can provide us with valuable information. Any employee of the federal government that has taken money from special interest groups will not keep their jobs. This is not only a smoke free zone but it is also a zone where no one accepts, or has accepted bribes from people or corporations. We all heard that promise before, but no matter who you are, if you are weak enough to take money to sway your opinion, then you are not welcome. Selling yourself, or your vote, is no better than the average whore on the street. It will not be tolerated. Also working for the new federal government is not a political position. The people that are receiving a government paycheck will leave their political preference at the door. Employees work for the citizens of the United States and not a political party. Over the next few weeks every federal employee will be re-screened. I am sure many will loose their jobs, and hopefully many will be kept. Many people will be unemployed because the size of government is going to be drastically reduced. I know of at least 66 Czars that are now out of work. The new government is going to be lean and mean. What we have to do, is to decide which programs and departments will be shut down. Some may be re-opened when we get a permanent government. Our job is to simplify things for the new administration, and the new leadership of the government. Excess spending has come to a halt.

When the stock market re-opens we need to make sure that it does not crash. Our economic committee is working on that with some of the best financial minds in the country. We will not bail out private corporations. We may invest in stock of a company, but that will only give us the same rights as a regular stockholder. No longer will we be in the automotive business. No longer are we in the banking business. Our days of sleeping with the pharmaceutical companies are over. Any company that attempts to sway, bribes, or secretly buys an elected, or appointed official, will be prosecuted. The term lobbying or lobbyist now deals with words, and not money or gifts. The people of this country must have confidence in what we are doing. Then we educate them, and turn the mess over to them to manage. Hopefully the idea of voting will have a new meaning. We will place term limits on all elected offices just like the presidency. The idea of becoming a politician to become rich will disappear. The desire to serve is what we will be looking for. If that still exists."

The next two men to speak to us are the Commanders of the Park Police and the Capital Police. They went over some general guidelines of what is expected and the procedures for the different properties of the Federal Government. The Capital Police is the policing agency that is in charge of protecting the United States Congress and the visitors. The Secret Service was not part of the discussion. They are concentrated on the White House and all the security measures concerning the safeguarding of the president. Even though we have no active president the planes, buildings, and other things need continued protection. This will keep them busy and out of our hair.

James again approached the bench and says, "Well it appears that we have our first crucial piece of business. At this time some of our fired legislatures, and our past president are trying to get support to take back their positions. We need to come up with a plan, or law, that will make them stop before someone gets hurt. Those with ideas can present them so that the members of the Supreme Court can take a look at them on their Constitutional merits. One idea that has been presented is this. We can enact a law, per say, like an Executive Order that states that all people involved in events that are taking place are forbidden to interfere with the new interim administration, and attempting to disrupt or change the present course would be considered treasonous. This could be legal because the interim government is not endangering the rights of the population or country. This also could be seen as a danger to the security of the country and the people of the United States. A gag order of some sort needs to be put in place where the angry past officials cannot talk about what is going on at this time, because it could incite a riot or other dangerous activity. Or we can simply gather them all up and lock them away for a time. Who would be interested in working on this matter with the members of the Supreme Court?"

There was a show of hands and so those who volunteered retired to a meeting room with members of the Court.

Here again, I was left in a situation where I had no political ambition, and really did not want to run a government. I have done what I came to do, even if it turned out to be very little. I get up and leave word that I am going to the Pentagon. I left and I am taken by the Pentagon where I stay for a few minutes. At this time there are no security threats, other than the people trying to cross the Mexican border. The border patrol and guard units are busy gathering up people and hauling them back to Mexico. The larger cities have the most infractions for breaking curfews. The rural areas are not a problem, and most likely are not even patrolled. So my work is done for the day.

I am taken back to my hotel and I see more movement in town than earlier. The streets are still heavily patrolled. At this point I didn't care. I just want a good meal and get some much-needed sleep, that has escaped me for the past few nights. If I get woke up again about North Korea, I will drop the bomb myself tonight. I convince myself that the reason I am not having a good time is because of my lack of sleep. So sleep is what I will get.

CHAPTER 8

▼

MY CAREER CHANGE

It is the forth day since the coup. In most areas martial law is being lifted and many Americans just want to get back to work. The stock market re-opened this morning and stocks actually rose on the initial market. In the previous days the Treasury Department had purchased a large quantity of stock and it seems to be working. It is the first day that the public will hear from a real person about what has happened and why. A brief description of what to look forward to will be relayed to the American people.

On my way to the Capitol, I can see numerous military helicopters in the air and an occasional F-16 fly by. A couple of large choppers from what looks like the Presidential Air Force, has landed in the street close to the Capitol building. As we pull up to the Capitol, there is James waiting for me. He has a smile from ear to ear and shakes my hand as I get out of the vehicle. He says, "Steve I am so glad you agreed to help us." I look at him in surprise and say, "I have not been asked to do anything yet James." He says, "Oh you will in a few minutes."

As we enter the building it is full of people. Many security personnel and military people are here doing their job. The mood is upbeat. We go upstairs to a large meeting room and I meet Veronica who was a former press secretary for a past president. James tells me that the members feel she will be a familiar face to talk with the country. She is non-threatening but to the point. She feels this is a major thing for America and wants to be part of it.

In reality what has happened is the very wealthy, along with the military has seized the moment under our plan, to take over the government to do what they wanted to do in the first place. We are just the bait in case things went wrong in the early planning stages. Our planners merged with the other planners to work together, to come up with viable plans for everything from the economy, security, foreign policy, and just anything that you can think of, that a government might run in to. I on the other hand have no skills at government work, nor do many others. I am just along for the ride to help with anything that is needed. The military is going out of their way to see that we serve some usefulness, instead of sitting on the sidelines. I appreciate that. The major problem is I had no clue on what to do. I am starting to become very bored.

It is fun getting to see all of the military things and to watch our military in action. But my duties only last two to three hours a day. I am not used to so much down time. I am ready to return to the world I know, and let the professionals finish the job. This time the voters will make the decisions. Until the elected representatives can be trusted to do their job of representing the people, there are penalties for them to stray to their own agendas, and major policy decisions will be voted on by the public. The fear of incarceration has made the past politicians afraid to confront the new interim administration. A few of them have been picked up by not abiding by the new orders from the new government. Under martial law they have no access to phones, attorneys, or any thing else that a person arrested under different times would have. That scared the others. Also military patrols watch the previous administration officials and make sure they did not violate the new standing orders. They have lost their phones and are monitored wherever they go. The surveillance teams on them do not make any attempt to be concealed. They stand right out side their front doors. We want them to know that we are watching them. All members of the Legislative Branch have their bank accounts frozen. The only money they have is what is in their pockets, or on their credit cards. And many credit cards did not work due to the communications blackouts. If I have my way, I would just as soon see many of them tied to a tree and shot. In some cases that is what some members are told. Violation of the law will result in termination. That got their attention. The threat of being taken to their areas of previous representation, and turned over to the very people they screwed, scared many of them. But there are some good politicians. They are few in numbers though.

As my mind is wandering James come up to me. He says, "The Joint Chiefs of Staff are impressed with you. They believe they can work with you in the capacity of Secretary of Defense. You will do as the rest of us by learning as you go along. You will get some of the best information about your duties from some of the best people available. The job will be perfect for you." I am almost speechless. I put my hand up to stop him from talking and say, "James, when I came on board, I told you that I did not want a position in the government. Especially not one that has to do with sending innocent young people to places where they might get killed. I have no desire to do that. I just wanted to remove the crooked politicians, and the military did that for me. Now I have no desires, except return back to my life, and watch as our country grows again. I really do appreciate the offer, but I would really like to go back home, and let people that know what they are doing continue the job of making America great again." James looks at me and says, "Well finish today and while at the Pentagon talk with the Admirals and Generals and then make the decision. Let them go over the details because the office of Secretary of Defense will not be the same as the previous administrations. It will be more of an administrative roll instead of a political role. You will be required to brief the new administration, and coordinate the intelligent communities to work with the military. More of a liaison position than it has been." I agree to continue through the day. But I pretty much have made my mind up.

I left for my daily briefing with the Pentagon. Upon arriving and after my briefing I ask the members of the Joint Chiefs to stay for a few minutes. I tell them of my feelings and my desire to return to the simple life I am used to. It is expressed to me that the new job will be far from simple, and expanded more on the duties of the Defense Secretary. I tell them, "Gentlemen I appreciate the offer. I am really not cut out to be in the political arena, nor do I really want to. I have no experience in matters of this type. I do not want to gamble with the lives of our soldiers. I do enjoy being here and especially getting to see the military work around the world in different arenas. But this job requires more ambition and awareness than what I have. I simply had a dream or at least an idea. I pushed that idea and it came true. Now the only dream I have is returning home and continue to live my life without interference from a corrupt government." They all understand. The position they offered will take a lot of time and create many headaches. It is time for me to take a more relaxed position. I want to go fishing.

CHAPTER 9

▼

THE END FOR ME AND THE BEGINNING FOR AMERICA

The next day I got my wish. I have been put on a plane and I am heading home. We are going to land at a private airstrip in Anthony, Florida. This way I can avoid any problem with the press and other people. I am going to meet with my wife and Jim, and we are going fishing. As we circled the airport I could see a truck with a boat on a trailer attached to the truck. This airport is the home of a famous movie artist and his wife. No one knows that I am arriving, so I should be able to leave the plane, get in the truck, and head out to some body of water and fish till we acquire supper. James has flown back home with me trying every mile to get me to change my mind, and take the new position. I am steadfast with my wants and declined his offer. In a few short months we have accomplished a great victory for everyone in America. Only in America can a few unimportant individuals plan and take over the government of the strongest country in the world.

We land and I get out of the plane and give my wife a big hug. It is really good to be back home. James says, "When you get bored with fishing, give me a call. I will find you a position that you will be happy with." I shook his hand and my reply is, "It has been an experience that I will never forget. Once it was all over my desire left at the same time. I will be content on watching you finish what we started." He held out a package and handed it to me. He said, "We shut down the non-profit organization and distributed the funds to everyone. You will have to report this to the IRS." He walked back to the plane and we watched it take off and head back to Washington D.C. Once the plane took off I had a strong sense of relief and a great feeling of being back home.

We went fishing that afternoon and my wife told me that I had many customers that have called wanting me to do some work for them. I am anxious to get back to work. Jim looks at me and asks, "Are you going to open that package to see what is in there?" I looked at it and say, "No not now. I want to enjoy the day. No telling what is in here." Jim replied, "Well I got one. I think that you will like what you find." I continue fishing. The strange thing about fishing for me is it does not matter if I catch anything. It is just being out in the open country relaxing. This is the greatest feeling about being free. This is what freedom is all about. Doing what you want to without interference from the government. It is a great day.

This evening my kids came over and brought the grandkids. Jim and his wife and son are here. We fixed a feast of Catfish, French fries, with coleslaw, and home made bread. The mood is fantastic and it is like nothing has happened. My son grabs the package and asks what was in it. I say, "I have no idea. But I would like not to have it opened until tomorrow. I am enjoying the evening and do not want anything to spoil my time tonight." So with that we had an enjoyable evening and again I got a good nights sleep.

In the following months I resumed my work as I have done before. However this time I do have a new truck from the proceeds that I got from our old corporation. What is different is I hurry home to watch the news of the day and the progress that our interim government is making. Most of America is happy with the outcome and is enjoying the change. With the building of new fuel refineries our fuel prices dropped in anticipation of an excess of supply. Gas is down to $1.50 a gallon. Natural gas is cheap and even our electricity prices have dropped substantially. It is actually cheap to live in the United States. Our news is accurate and those that exaggerate the facts are not long in the career of broadcasting. My wife and I finally get to take a real vacation thanks to the money I have received.

The country is gearing up for the most important election of the history of the United States. A few new rules have been implemented for the election. You have to be a citizen with proof of identification. You cannot be a convicted felon. It is illegal for anyone to approach an individual in line to vote except for the people at the voting place. No more special interest groups trying to sway a person on their vote. There are places that everyone can go to get information on the people running for office, and correct information about bills and legislation that is being voted on. The rules of becoming a candidate have changed. Many of the old politicians cannot run again under the new rules. A Congressman can only serve for two terms. A public nonpartisan committee was formed to monitor elected officials and if needed remove them from office. If the infraction that causes their removal is of a criminal nature, then they will be arrested and prosecuted. Lobbying is almost a capital offense. One who bribes an elected official is given such a harsh sentence that it is less punishment to commit manslaughter than bribery. And with the new procedures in prison that is changed, life is not fun at all. It is not a luxury resort where gang members rule the roost. Their life has changed dramatically and prison is no longer a place that a criminal does not fear. When a person enters prison they loose all civil rights. You are a criminal and are treated like one. No more civil suits filed from prison. It is a new world for the criminals. And many politicians are headed there.

A large number of our previous politicians are going to be prosecuted. Many are being prosecuted from existing laws concerning illegal acceptance of money. This was mostly overlooked from the previous administration, since they all accepted bribes at one point in their political career. The lobbyist that gave them the money, are also on their way to prison. Most of the inmates of prison have heard the reason their life has turned bad while being in prison, is due to these people that accepted, and gave money intended to change a vote for money. This angered inmates all over the country. The life expectancy of one of these individuals in prison cannot be accurately calculated. Some have had early accidents while in prison.

Our military has pretty well sent a message to the world. It is a simple message. Simply stated it says, "Don't screw with us." The military has taught everyone a good lesson. It is that a country does not have to be an ally of the United States to be treated fairly. We will not mess with the workings of another country, as long as certain civil rights violations do not occur. And then it will take an act of Congress to get approval for involvement. We are once again respected around the world.

My idea of making a law that everyone one reaching the age of 18 will spend two years in the military is to be voted on during the new election. Much of my idea has been fine tuned, and more Americans are for it then I have anticipated. The men and women that are having to join the military are not so happy, but many minorities see this as a great opportunity to get out of poverty and have a chance to make something out of their life. One can imagine that many welfare recipients are not happy with the proposal. With the best intentions in mind, you just can't please everyone.

The flow of illegal immigrants has stopped at our borders. With the military patrolling our borders, millions of dollars are being saved on medical expenses and other expenditures that are involved helping people that have entered our country illegally. The new people running for office have vowed to help Mexico get rid of their criminal activity, and are helping them create an economy that will employ their people. Aid for other country's is being evaluated. No longer will we give money to a country that is wealthy and is capable of giving their own population aid. No longer will we give rogue governments money that is radical and dangerous. The new belief is to get Americans off the street, out of the slums, making them productive. Once that task is accomplished then we will look at other nations. But our country has a lot of work to do first.

The task of our government, and more importantly our people, is to make sure that bribery of an official never takes place again. Special interest groups will have to be accurate about the words they say, and heavy punishments will be dealt to those that intimidate others. This is especially aimed at the unions. Political offices will no longer be a place where a politician can become rich. And no politician can have interest where they will benefit off of legislation that comes up for a vote. In other words, public service will go back to being a position that will be very rewarding, but not profitable. This is up to America, and by using the court system and voting booths, hopefully this story of fiction will never turn into reality.